PAINTED LADIES

THE SPENSER NOVELS

THE JESSE STONE NOVELS

THE SUNNY RANDALL NOVELS

THE VIRGIL COLE/ EVERETT HITCH NOVELS

ALSO BY ROBERT B. PARKER

PAINTED LADIES

Robert B. Parker

G. P. PUTNAM'S SONS

New York

G. P. PUTNAM'S SONS
Publishers Since 1838
Published by the Penguin Group
Penguin Group (USA) Inc., 375 Hudson Street, New York, New York
10014, USA • Penguin Group (Canada), 90 Eglinton Avenue East, Suite 700,
Toronto, Ontario M4P 2Y3, Canada (a division of Pearson Penguin Canada Inc.) • Penguin
Books Ltd, 80 Strand, London WC2R 0RL, England • Penguin Ireland,
25 St Stephen's Green, Dublin 2, Ireland (a division of Penguin Books Ltd) • Penguin
Group (Australia), 250 Camberwell Road, Camberwell, Victoria 3124, Australia
(a division of Pearson Australia Group Pty Ltd) • Penguin Books India Pvt Ltd,
11 Community Centre, Panchsheel Park, New Delhi–110 017, India • Penguin
Group (NZ), 67 Apollo Drive, Rosedale, North Shore 0632, New Zealand (a division
of Pearson New Zealand Ltd) • Penguin Books (South Africa) (Pty) Ltd,
24 Sturdee Avenue, Rosebank, Johannesburg 2196, South Africa

Penguin Books Ltd, Registered Offices: 80 Strand, London WC2R 0RL, England

This is a work of fiction. Names, characters, places, and incidents either are the product of the author's imagination or are used fictitiously, and any resemblance to actual persons, living or dead, businesses, companies, events, or locales is entirely coincidental.

While the author has made every effort to provide accurate telephone numbers and Internet addresses at the time of publication, neither the publisher nor the author assumes any responsibility for errors, or for changes that occur after publication. Further, the publisher does not have any control over and does not assume any responsibility for author or third-party websites or their content.

For Joan: live art

PAINTED LADIES

1

My first client of the day (and of the week, truth be known) came into my office on the Tuesday after Thanksgiving and sat in one of my client chairs. He was medium-height and slim, wearing a brown tweed suit, a blue paisley bow tie, and a look of satisfaction.

"You're Spenser," he said.

"Yes, I am," I said.

"I am Dr. Ashton Prince," he said.

He handed me a card, which I put on my desk.

"How nice," I said.

"Excuse me?"

"What can I do for you, Dr. Prince."

"I am confronted with a matter of extreme sensitivity," he said.

I nodded.

"May I count on your discretion?" he said.

"Sure," I said.

"I'm serious," he said.

"I can tell," I said.

He frowned slightly. Less in disapproval than in uncertainty.

"Well," he said, "may I?"

"Count on my discretion?"

"Yes!"

"At the moment, I don't have anything to be discreet about," I said. "But I would be if I did."

He stared at me for a moment, then smiled.

"I see," he said. "You're attempting to be funny."

"'Attempting'?" I said.

"No matter," Prince said. "But I need to know you are capable of taking my issues seriously."

"I'd be in a better position to assess that," I said, "if you told me what your issues were."

He nodded slowly to himself.

"I was warned that you were given to self-amusement," he said. "I guess there's no help for it. I am a professor of art history at Walford University. And I am a forensic art consultant in matters of theft and forgery."

And pleased about it.

"Is there such a matter before us?" I said.

He took in some air and let it out audibly.

"There is," he said.

"And it requires discretion," I said.

"Very much."

"You'll get all I can give you," I said.

"All you can give me?"

"Anything," I said, "that your best interest, and my self-regard, will allow."

"Your 'self-regard'?"

"I try not to do things that make me think ill of myself."

"My God," Prince said. "I mean, that's a laudable goal, I suppose. But you are a private detective."

"All the more reason for vigilance," I said.

He took another deep breath. He nodded slowly.

"There is a painting," he said, "by a seventeenth-century Dutch artist named Frans Hermenszoon."

"*Lady with a Finch*," I said.

"How on earth did you know that?" Prince said.

"Only Hermenszoon painting I've ever heard of."

"He painted very few," Prince said. "Hermenszoon died at age twenty-six."

"Young," I said.

"Rather," Prince said. "But *Lady with a Finch* was a masterpiece. Is a masterpiece. It belongs to the Hammond Museum. And last week it was stolen."

"Heard from the thieves?" I said.

"Yes."

"Ransom?" I said.

"Yes."

"And if you bring any cops in, they'll destroy the painting," I said.

"Yes."

"So what do you want from me?" I said.

"The Hammond wants the whole matter handled entirely, ah, sotto voce. They have asked me to handle the exchange."

"The money for the painting," I said.

"Yes, and I am, frankly, uneasy. I want protection."

"Me," I said.

"The chief of the Walford campus police asked a friend at the Boston Police Department on my behalf, and you were recommended."

"I'm very popular there," I said.

"Will you do it?"

"Okay," I said.

"Like that?" Prince said.

"Sure," I said.

"What do you charge?"

I told him. He raised his eyebrows.

"Well," he said. "I'm sure they will cover it."

"The museum."

"Yes," he said. "And if they won't cover it all, I'll make up the difference out of pocket."

"Generous," I said.

"You're being ironic," he said.

"It is you I'm protecting," I said.

"I know," he said. "The painting, too. It is not merely a

brilliant piece of art, though that would be enough. It is also the expression of a distant life, cut sadly short."

"I'll do my best," I said.

"Which I'm told," Prince said, "is considerable."

I nodded.

"'Tis," I said.

2

Susan and Pearl were spending the weekend with me. It was Saturday morning and the three of us were out for a mid-morning stroll in the Public Garden. Pearl was off the leash so she could dash about and annoy the pigeons, which she was doing, while Susan and I watched proudly.

"So you are going to make this exchange Monday morning?" Susan said.

"Yep."

"How do you feel about it?" she said.

"I am, as you know, fearless."

"Mostly," Susan said.

"'Mostly'?"

Susan smiled and shook her head.

"What's bothering you about it?" she said.

"An exchange like this," I said, "they gotta be sure they get the money before they give you the painting. You gotta be sure you get the painting before you give them the money. They gotta be sure that once they give up the painting the cops don't swoop in and bust them."

"Difficult," Susan said.

"And their side gets to call the shots," I said.

"Which you don't like," Susan said.

"Which I don't like," I said.

"Ducks," Susan said. "You don't like anyone else calling the shots on what tie to wear."

"Except you," I said.

Susan smiled.

"Of course," she said. "Always *except me*."

A group of pigeons was pecking at some popcorn that had been thrown on the ground for them. Pearl chased them off and ate the popcorn. A mature woman in a leopard-skin coat stood up from the bench where the pigeons had gathered and walked toward us.

"Madam," she said, "control your dog. That popcorn is intended for the pigeons."

Susan smiled.

"Survival of the fittest," she said.

The woman frowned.

She said, "Don't be flippant, young woman."

"Yikes," I murmured.

Susan turned slowly toward the woman.

"Oh, kiss my ass," Susan said.

The woman took a half-step back. Her face reddened. She opened her mouth, and closed it, and turned and marched away.

"They teach you 'kiss my ass' at Harvard?" I said.

"No," Susan said. "I learned that from you. . . . Pearl likes popcorn."

"At least she called you 'young woman,'" I said.

Susan was glaring after the woman.

"By her standards," Susan said.

Suddenly Pearl stopped scavenging the popcorn and stood motionless, her ears pricked, as if she were pointing. Which she wasn't. She was staring.

Coming toward us was a yellow Lab with a massive head and a broad chest. He was wagging his tail majestically as he trotted toward us, as if he was one hell of a dog and proud of it. He stopped about a foot in front of Pearl, and they looked at each other. They sniffed each other. They circled each other, sniffing as they went. Pearl didn't suffer fools gladly, so I stayed close. In case. Then Pearl stretched her front paws out and dropped her chest and raised her hind end. The Lab did the same. Then Pearl rose up and tore around in a circle. The Lab went after her. The circle widened, and pretty soon the two dogs were racing around the whole of the Public Garden. Occasionally they would stop to put their heads down and tails up. Then they would race around some more. An attractive blonde woman was standing near us, watching.

"Your dog?" Susan said.

"Yes," she said. "Otto."

"Mine is Pearl," Susan said. "They seem to be getting along."

The woman smiled.

"Or would if they slowed down," she said.

We watched as the flirtation continued. The two dogs began to roll on the ground, mouthing each other in make-believe bites, unsuccessfully trying to pin each other down with a front paw.

"Do you bring Pearl here regularly?" Otto's mom said.

"Quite often," Susan said.

"We're in from New York, staying across the park."

Otto's mom nodded toward the Four Seasons.

"They seem so taken with each other," she said. "Do you have a card or something? I could call you. Maybe they could meet again while we're here?"

"Please," Susan said. "Pearl will be thrilled."

Susan gave her a card.

"Otto doesn't mind that Pearl is spayed?" I said.

"Otto's been neutered," his mom said.

"Men!" Susan said to me. "This is love, not sex."

"Both are nice," I said.

The two dogs stood, panting, tails wagging, looking at each other.

"You should know," Susan said.

3

Today, Prince had on a gray tweed suit and a polka-dot bow tie.

"We're supposed to go west on Route Two," he said when I got in his car. "They'll call me on my cell phone and tell me where to go next."

The car was an entry-level Volvo sedan, which was a little tight for me.

"Do they know I'm along?" I said.

"I told them I was bringing a friend because I was afraid to come alone," he said.

"And?"

"They said you'd have to stay in the car and not get in the way."

I nodded.

"Do you have a gun?" he said.

"Of course," I said.

"Have you ever used it?" he said.

"Yes."

"To shoot somebody?"

"Mostly I use the front sight to pick my teeth," I said.

He smiled a little.

We drove west on Storrow along the river. It was bright today, and pretty chilly. But the boat crews were hard at it, as they would be until the river froze. To our left, we passed the former Braves Field, now a BU athletic field. The old stucco entrance was still there on Gaffney Street, and maybe vestiges of the right-field Jury Box. An elevated section of the Mass Pike ran above the railroad tracks outside of left field.

"When the Braves played there," I said, "an outfielder named Danny Litwhiler is alleged to have hit a ball that cleared the left-field wall and landed in a freight car headed to Buffalo, thus hitting the longest measurable home run in baseball history."

"I'm sorry, I don't believe I understand what you're saying," Prince said.

"Never mind," I said.

No one was tailing us as we went west on Route 2. Or if they were, they were better than I was. Which seemed unlikely to me. Probably had somebody set up to spot us when we got to a certain point, and then they'd call. I looked for a spotter. But I didn't see one.

We were approaching Route 128, which in this section

was also known to be Interstate Route 95. The phone rang. Prince answered and listened.

After a minute of listening he said, "Okay."

He looked at me.

"Cross the overpass on One twenty-eight and turn around on the other side and start back, driving slowly," he said.

I glanced back. The spotter was probably standing on one of the cross-street overpasses. We crossed above 128 and drove on into Lincoln until we found a place to turn around, and then we drove toward where we'd been. Prince had the cell phone to his ear. He nodded.

"Stop under the first overpass we come to," he said. "Okay . . . I get out with the money . . . Okay . . . And climb up with it and stand in the middle of the bridge."

Prince looked at me.

"You're to stay in the car or there's no deal."

I nodded.

We pulled over to the side under the first overpass. He swallowed audibly and got out of the car. I reached in back and got the suitcase full of money, and handed it out to Prince.

"Break a leg," I said.

He nodded and turned and lugged the big suitcase slowly up the ramp behind us. A suitcase full of money is heavy.

From where I sat, directly beneath the overpass, I couldn't even see the swap. I put the windows down and shut off the engine, and listened intently. Cars went by on Route 2. Above me I thought I heard one. Maybe it stopped in the middle. Maybe its door opened. About thirty seconds later, maybe it shut. And maybe the car drove off. I waited. Silence. I looked back at the slope that supported the down ramp. In a moment I saw Prince scrambling down, carrying a surprisingly small paper-wrapped square. Maybe this was going to work out.

It didn't. Just as he came into sight, the package exploded and blew him and itself into a mess.

4

I was sitting in the backseat of Captain Healy's unmarked Mass State police cruiser. Healy sat in front behind the wheel, and beside him was an assistant DA from Middlesex named Kate Quaggliosi. Kate had a fine body and olive skin. Her hair was blond.

"Weren't too useful, were you?" Kate said.

"I didn't actually help them," I said.

"Didn't do much to hinder them," Kate said.

"Don't overstate," I said.

"Okay," she said. "You did nothing to hinder them."

"That's more accurate," I said.

"Good," Kate said. "Glad we got that settled."

She looked at Healy.

"You know this guy?" she said.

"I do," he said. "He's very annoying."

"I noticed," Kate said.

"But if he couldn't have saved this situation, no one could have."

"Gee, Captain," I said.

Healy looked at me.

"Shut up," he said.

He looked back at Kate.

"And trust me," Healy said to her, "he does not like it that this went down this way on his watch. And he won't let it go until he makes it right."

"In whose opinion," she said.

"His," Healy said. "Only one matters to him."

"Susan's opinion matters," I said.

"Who?" Kate said.

"Girl of my dreams," I said.

"So you might as well learn to deal with him now," Healy said. "Because everywhere we turn on this, from here on in, we're going to bump into him."

"Well," she said. "Annoying *and* persistent."

"And sometimes helpful," I said.

She looked at Healy. He nodded.

"I find it's better to work with him than fight him," Healy said.

"You've told us everything you know," she said to me.

"Yep."

"It's not very much," she said.

"I don't know very much," I said.

She smiled slightly.

"In this case?" she said. "Or are you speaking more generally."

"Probably both," I said.

"Modest, too," she said.

"I have much to be modest about," I said.

"Certainly true," she said, "since I've known you. You have any questions for us?"

"You really blonde?" I said.

"With a name like Quaggliosi?" she said.

"I thought maybe it was your married name."

"My husband's name is Henderson. Henderson, Lake, Taylor, and Caldwell, attorneys at law. He makes money; I do good."

"So you're not really blonde," I said.

"You'll never know," she said. "But thanks for asking."

5

Healy drove me back to my office.

"They didn't improvise that bomb on the spur of the moment," he said.

"No," I said.

"They planned to kill him all along," Healy said.

"Or at least before they left for the exchange," I said.

"Why?" Healy said.

"You don't know, either?" I said.

"No."

"You're a captain," I said.

"I know," Healy said. "It's embarrassing."

"Homicide commander," I said.

"I know," Healy said. "Why blow up the picture?"

"It's a painting," I said.

"Sure," Healy said. "Why blow up the picture?"

"Maybe it's not the painting," I said. "Enough of it left to tell?"

"Crime scene people will let us know," Healy said. "But I doubt it."

"He gave them the money and came down the hill with it," I said.

"When he was up there they could have pointed a gun at him and told him to take it," Healy said.

"True. Maybe he was in on it," I said.

"And once they got the money," Healy said, "they aced him so he couldn't tell anyone?"

"One less split of the ransom," I said.

Healy grinned.

"A positive side effect," he said. "How much was the ransom?"

"Didn't tell me."

Healy nodded.

"Who supplied the dough?" he said.

"Hammond Museum, I assume."

"Their money, or insurance?" Healy said.

"Don't know."

"If it was insurance, they'll be climbing all over this thing as well," Healy said.

"As well as what?"

"As well as you," Healy said.

"Except I'll be trying to catch the perps," I said. "And the insurance guys will be trying not to pay."

"There's that," Healy said.

We went past the Red Line MBTA station, past the shopping center, around Fresh Pond Circle and the reservoir, heading toward the river. In the bright December sunshine, the reservoir looked encouragingly blue and fresh.

"I got hired to do one thing," I said. "Keep him safe while he collected the painting."

Healy nodded.

"You did everything else okay," he said.

"Thanks," I said.

Healy shrugged.

"I don't know what you could have done," Healy said.

"I don't, either," I said. "But whatever it was, I didn't do it."

"They outthought you," Healy said.

"It's part of what makes me mad," I said.

"They controlled the situation," Healy said. "It was a mismatch."

"I guess."

"Your pride's hurt," Healy said.

"This is what I do," I said. "I can't do it, where am I?"

"Where everybody is sometimes," Healy said. "You looking for revenge?"

"No," I said. "I barely knew the guy, and if I knew him better, I probably wouldn't have enjoyed him."

"You're looking to even it up," Healy said.

"Something like that," I said.

"I know," Healy said.

"I know you do," I said.

We went around the head of the Charles and onto Soldiers Field Road past Harvard Stadium on the Boston side of the river.

"Some guys become cops because they get to carry a piece and order people around," Healy said. "And some people do it because they like the work, and think it's important."

"Like you," I said.

Healy nodded.

"And you," he said. "Except you can't work in a command structure."

"I'm with Susan," I said.

"Besides that," Healy said.

"So you don't have a problem," I said, "with me looking into this."

"Nope," Healy said. "You're nearly as good as you think you are, and you'll do things I'm not allowed to do."

"Damned command structure again," I said.

"It has its uses," Healy said. "Not every cop is as pure of heart as you are."

"Or as much fun," I said.

"Fun," Healy said. "Long as you are fun on the right side of things, I got no problem with you."

"Nor I with you," I said.

"I am the right side of things," Healy said.

"Ah," I said. "That's where it is."

6

The Hammond Museum was a big gray stone building located in Chestnut Hill, halfway between Boston College and the Longwood Cricket Club. It had a gambrel roof and Palladian windows, and looked like one of those baronial cottages on the oceanfront in Newport.

I parked next to the museum in a slot marked *Museum Staff Only*. In the summer the grounds were richly landscaped. But now as we slid into December, the landscape was leafless and stiff.

The entry hall went all the way to a stained-glass window in back of the building. The hall was vaulted, two stories high, and sparsely hung with some Italian Renaissance paintings. Women in the Italian Renaissance were apparently very zaftig.

The director's office was on the third floor, with a swell view of some dark, naked trees that in summer would doubtless offer a rich, green ambiance. The office itself was sparse and sort of streamlined-looking, with light maple furniture and some Picasso sketches on the wall.

There were two men in the room, one behind a desk that looked like a conference table and the other sitting across from the desk on a couch. The guy at the desk stood when I came in and stepped around his desk and put out his hand.

"Mark Richards," he said. "I'm the museum director."

We shook hands.

"This is Morton Lloyd," Richards said. "He's our attorney."

I shook his hand.

"What a damned mess this has all turned into," Richards said.

"Especially for Ashton Prince," I said.

"I know," he said. "Poor Ash. How too bad."

"He gave you money," the lawyer said. "To protect him."

"He did," I said.

"Can't say I think you've earned it."

"I haven't," I said, and took an envelope from my inside pocket and tossed it onto Richards's desk.

"What's this," he said.

"The check he gave me," I said. "It's drawn on the museum account."

"You didn't cash it?"

"No," I said.

"And you're returning it?"

"Yes," I said.

"Because you were unable to protect him," Richards said.

"I didn't earn it," I said.

Richards nodded. He looked at the lawyer.

"He's right," the lawyer said. "He didn't."

Richards nodded again.

"Thank you," he said to me.

He put the envelope on top of his desk, and put a small stone carving of a pregnant woman on top of it to hold it still.

"Did you come here simply to return your fee?" the lawyer said.

"No, I'm looking for information," I said.

"About what?" the lawyer said.

"About the kidnapped painting and the ransom payment and Ashton Prince and anything else you can tell me," I said.

"You're planning to investigate this business?" the lawyer said.

"Yes," I said.

"And who's paying you?" the lawyer said.

"Pro bono."

"We've already spoken with the police, and with the insurance people," the lawyer said.

I nodded.

"I see no reason we should speak to you," the lawyer said.

I looked at Richards. He shrugged.

"I understand that you are trying to make good on something," Richards said. "And I am sympathetic. But I feel that the museum should be guided by our attorney."

I nodded.

"Been working out great so far," I said.

"Just what do you mean by that?" the lawyer said.

"Hell," I said. "I have no idea."

And I turned and walked out of the office without closing the door. . . . That showed 'em.

7

Healy came into my office with two large coffees and a dozen doughnuts. He put one coffee on my desk and offered me a doughnut.

"A bribe?" I said.

"Authentic cop food," Healy said.

"Oh, boy," I said. "Two of these babies and I'll run out and give somebody a ticket."

"Thought I might come by this morning and compare notes," Healy said.

"Which means you haven't got much and you're wondering if I do," I said.

"You want the doughnuts or not," Healy said.

"Okay," I said. I took a significant bite. "I know nothing."

"Lot of that going around," Healy said.

"You talk to the museum people?" I said.

"Yep, Richards, the director, and his man Lloyd, the lawyer," Healy said. "You?"

"Same two," I said.

"And?"

"They wouldn't tell me anything," I said. "How'd you do."

"No better," Healy said. "And I'm a captain."

"Did you tell them that?" I said.

"They seemed unimpressed."

"You know who the insurance company is?"

"I did get that," Healy said. "Shawmut."

"Way to go, Captain."

"Their home office is here," Healy said. "Berkeley Street, corner of Columbus. Right up from you."

"I know the building," I said. "Got the name of an investigator or somebody?"

"They call them claim-resolution specialists."

"Of course they do," I said.

"Called over there," Healy said. "They tell me the claims-resolution specialist has not yet been assigned."

"Who'd you talk with," I said.

"Head of claims resolution, woman named Winifred Minor."

"How about Prince?" I said.

"Professor at Walford University," Healy said. "Married, no kids, lived in Cambridge."

"Cambridge," I said. "There's a surprise. You talk with the wife?"

"Distraught," Healy said. "Doctor's care. So no, we haven't talked to her."

"She use his name?" I said.

"She's a poet," Healy said.

"So she doesn't use his name," I said.

"No," Healy said. "Her name is Rosalind Wellington."

"Wow," I said.

"You read a lot," Healy said. "You ever heard of her?"

"No," I said. "But maybe she doesn't know who I am, either."

"I'd bet on it," Healy said.

"What about Prince?" I said. "Anything?"

"We interviewed some colleagues at Walford. Nobody seems to know much about him. Quiet guy, minded his own business."

"Talk to students?"

"A few," Healy said. "Ordinary teacher, easy grader, nothing remarkable."

"How'd he end up consulting on the art theft?"

"I asked that question," Healy said. "They were a little evasive, but it appears that Lawyer Lloyd recommended him."

I fumbled around in my desk drawer and took out the card Prince had given me at our first meeting. It said *Ashton Prince, Ph.D.,* and a phone number. I passed it to Healy.

"He told me he was a forensic consultant," I said.

"That's his home phone," Healy said.

"Heavens," I said. "No wonder you made captain. You know if he had an office or anything?"

"None that we can find," Healy said.

"What about Lawyer Lloyd?" I said.

"Morton Lloyd," Healy said. "Tort specialist. Works for the museum pro bono."

"He legit?" I said.

"Far's we can tell," Healy said.

"He got an office?"

"Yeah, on Batterymarch," Healy said. "Lloyd and Leiter."

"He tell you that?" I said.

"No," Healy said.

"Everybody is holding their cards right in close to their chest," I said.

"Yep."

"Whaddya think that's about?" I said.

"I think the picture is still out there," Healy said.

"That's what I think," I said.

8

Shawmut Insurance Company was very handy, so when Healy left, I went over there. It was a medium-size brick-and-granite building, built in the time when people seemed to care about how buildings looked. There was an arched entrance on Columbus, and a smaller one on Berkeley. Next to it there was a hotel that used to be Boston police headquarters.

I wanted the full experience, so I went around the corner onto Columbus and went in the granite arched main entrance. Inside was a big old lobby that rose several stories. Opposite the entry was a black iron elevator cage. I asked the security guy at the desk for Winifred Minor and was sent, via the black iron elevator, to the third floor.

The third floor was open and full of desks, except along

the Columbus Avenue side, where a series of half-partitioned cubicles marched in a fearful symmetry. The one where Winifred Minor had her desk had a higher partition than those on either side of her. Status! There was one at the far end that not only had a floor-to-ceiling partition but also a secretary outside. Deification. I stuck my head in the opening of Winifred Minor's cubicle and rapped gently on the outer edge.

"Yes?"

I stepped in.

"My name's Spenser," I said. "I believe you talked with Captain Healy on the phone. I'm just stopping by to follow up."

She looked at me as though she might be going to buy me.

"Spenser," she said, and wrote in a small notebook that was open in front of her.

I nodded and put a little wattage into my killer smile. She survived it.

"First name?" she said.

I told her. She wrote that down in her little notebook. Then she looked straight at me and spoke. Her voice was very clear, and her speech was precise.

"I have nothing to say."

"You know," I said, "I don't, either. These first meetings are awkward as hell, aren't they."

She leaned back a little and folded her arms. She frowned, though it wasn't an angry frown. She looked good. She had thick black hair that she wore long. She had Tina Fey glasses and was wearing a white shirt and a fitted black tunic with brass buttons. I couldn't see what she was wearing below that because the desk was in the way. But what showed of her was very well made up, very pulled together, and hot.

"Once we get to know each other," I said, "we'll be chattering like a couple of schoolgirls, but the first moments are always hard."

"Well," she said in her clear, precise way, "you are not the standard cop."

I smiled and tilted my head a little in obvious modesty.

"I know," I said.

She looked at me some more. I dialed my smile up a little higher. She smiled back at me.

"Does this crap usually work for you?" she said.

I grinned.

"Sometimes," I said.

"Well," she said. "This is one of those times. Sit down. Tell me what you need."

Magnified by the fancy glasses, her dark eyes seemed even bigger than they probably were. She knew they were a good feature. She let them rest steadily on me. She didn't blink. She sat and looked and waited.

"Okay," I said. "Right from the beginning, I want there to be no secrets between us."

She didn't smile. But something sort of glittered in her eyes.

"I'm not a cop. I'm a private detective."

"You were adroit at letting me think you were a cop, without actually saying so."

"Thank you," I said.

"So who is your client," she said.

"Nobody," I said. "I'm the guy who was supposed to protect Ashton Prince when he delivered the, ah, ransom."

"And you are not satisfied with your performance," she said.

"No."

"What I know of the event, I don't see what you could have done differently," she said.

I didn't answer.

"So," she said, "the, ah, deceased is, in a sense, your client."

"You could say so, I suppose."

"What do you need from me?" she said.

"I'd love to know who's working on it from your end," I said.

"Me," she said.

"Bingo," I said. "First at bat. What can you tell me?"

"Nothing," she said. "Except there is a lot here you do not understand and cannot find out. You did the best you could. It was not enough. Were I you, I would leave it and move on."

"Can't do that," I said.

She nodded.

"Were you ever a police officer?" she said.

"Yes."

"Did you clear every case?"

"No," I said.

"Was that always because there wasn't enough evidence?"

"No."

"Occasionally, was it because too many important people did not want the case cleared?"

"Yes."

She was still leaning back in her chair with her arms folded. She nodded slowly. And kept nodding for a while.

"You ever a cop?" I said.

"I was with the Bureau for a while. Before that I was with the Secret Service."

"Protection?" I said.

"Yes."

"Why are you here?"

"I have children," she said.

"Husband?" I said.

"No," she said.

I nodded again.

"This job is regular hours," she said. "Better pay, and good benefits."

"And fun as hell," I said.

"When you have children and you are a single parent, fun is not part of the equation."

"Too bad," I said. "Can you tell me anything about any important people who might not want this case cleared?"

"No," she said.

I nodded.

"Point me in any direction?"

"No."

"You going to settle the claim?" I said.

"Too early to say."

We sat and looked at each other. She knew I wasn't going to take her advice. I knew she wasn't going to tell me anything.

"Your first name is Winifred?" I said.

"Yes."

"You don't look like a Winifred to me," I said.

"Nor to me," she said. "But which nickname would you prefer: Winnie or Fred?"

I smiled.

"Good-bye, Winifred," I said.

"Good-bye."

"Thanks for the advice."

"Which you won't take," she said.

"No."

She stood and came around the desk. She was wearing a skirt. Her legs were great. I stood. She put out her hand. I took it.

"Be careful," she said.

"Within reason," I said.

"Most of us, I suppose, do what we must, more than what we should," she said.

"Sometimes they overlap," I said.

"Perhaps," she said.

We shook hands, and I left. I was glad her legs were great.

9

It was raining and very windy. I had swiveled my chair around so I could look out my office window and watch the weather. As I was watching, there was a sort of self-effacing little tap on my office door. I swiveled around and said, "Come in."

The door opened about halfway, and a woman peeked in with her head tilted sideways. She had gray-brown hair, and she was wearing glasses with metal frames that looked sort of government-issue.

"Mr. Spenser?"

"Yes."

"May I come in?"

"Sure."

"I don't have an appointment," she said.

I smiled.

"I can squeeze you in," I said.

"I could come back," she said.

I stood up.

"Come in," I said. "Talk to me. I'm lonely."

She opened the door all the way and sort of darted through it, as if she didn't want to waste my time. I gestured for her to sit in a chair in front of my desk. She scooted to it and sat down. She was carrying a green rain poncho.

"May I put this on the floor?" she said. "I don't want to get your furniture wet."

"Sure."

She was kind of thin, and seemed to be flat-chested, although the bulky brown sweater she was wearing didn't allow a definitive judgment. Her face was small. Her skin was pale. I saw no evidence of makeup. She put the poncho on the floor and perched on the front edge of the chair with her knees together. She smoothed her ankle-length tan skirt down over them. She folded her hands in her lap for a moment, then unfolded them and rested them on the arms of her chair. Then she refolded them in her lap and sat forward.

"Sometimes I think loneliness describes the human condition," she said.

"Actually," I said, "I'm not lonely. I was just being, ah, lighthearted."

She nodded. We sat. Now that she had settled on what to do with her hands, she was motionless. I smiled. She looked down at her hands.

"I'm Rosalind Wellington," she said. "Ashton Prince . . . was my husband."

"I'm sorry for your loss," I said.

She nodded and looked at her hands some more.

"They told me you were with him when he died," she said.

"Yes," I said.

She was silent. I waited. I could hear the rain splattering on my window behind me.

"I have to know everything," she said.

"About?" I said.

"I am an artist, a poet. Images are how I think. Perhaps even how I exist. I have to see every image of his death before I can internalize it."

"Oh," I said.

"I have to be able to imagine everything," she said.

"What do you know?" I said.

"He is dead," she said. "Can I say it? Murdered! With a bomb."

"What else do you want to know," I said.

"Everything. I need to know what the sky looked like. I need the smell of the roadside, the song of the bomb. Did it startle the birds and make them fly up? Did insects react in the grass? Was there any reaction from the universe, or did the ship sail calmly on? I need to know. I need to see and hear and smell in order to feel. I need to feel in order to make something of this. To create something that will rise above."

All this time she had not looked up from her hands.

"He never knew what hit him," I said. "He didn't suffer."

"Thank you," she said. "But give me details. I need images. The police tried to spare me. And I suppose in their earthbound way, they were trying to be kind. But they don't understand. Was he badly disfigured?"

I took in a deep breath and said, "He was blown into small bits unrecognizable as anything except blood spatters."

She hunched her shoulders and put her hands to her face and kept them there while she breathed deeply.

Finally she said through her muffling hands, "Please go on."

I told her everything I could. I didn't like it. I didn't know if she was heroic or crazy. But it wasn't a judgment I needed to make. People grieve in their own ways, and she had the right to get what she thought she needed. She listened with her face in her hands until I was done.

"That's all there is," I said.

She raised her face, dry-eyed, and nodded.

"If I can make a great poem out of Ash's death," she said, "then perhaps he can, in his way, live on in the poem, and perhaps I can, too."

"I hope so," I said.

She nodded sort of absently. Then she stood without another word and left.

10

It was very odd," I said to Susan.

We were sitting on her couch with our feet up on her coffee table. She was drinking some pink champagne I had brought. I was drinking some scotch and soda that she kept for me. We had conspired on a lamb stew for supper, and it was simmering in a handsome pot on Susan's stove. Pearl was in the bedroom, asleep on Susan's bed, which made it easier to sit with my arm around Susan. I was pretty sure that when supper was served, Pearl would present herself.

"Very," Susan said.

The conspiracy on the lamb stew had been Susan putting out the pots and the cutting board and the utensils, and me cooking it while she sat at her kitchen counter and watched appreciatively.

"She even alluded to 'Musée des Beaux Arts,'" I said.

"The Auden poem?" Susan said. "How'd she do that?"

"She wanted to know if, in effect, the universe took note of the murder or if the boat 'sailed calmly on.'"

"Wow," Susan said. "Isn't that the poem which says 'the torturer's horse scratches his innocent behind on a tree'? Or something like that."

I leaned forward on the couch and took the champagne from the ice bucket and poured her a little more of it.

"It is," I said.

"Perhaps Auden knew things that Rosalind doesn't," Susan said.

"'About suffering, they were never wrong, the Old Masters,'" I said.

"Can you recite the whole poem?" Susan said.

"I believe I can," I said.

"Don't," she said.

"You know," I said, "she never asked me why I hadn't done a better job of protecting him. She never asked if I knew who did it or if I thought we could catch them. Just wanted to experience it secondhand so she could make something out of it."

"Many people would have," Susan said.

"Many people," I said.

"How'd she feel to you?"

"I know her husband has recently been murdered. I know grief makes people odd sometimes," I said. "But she seemed to be dramatizing herself. She didn't cry or, as far as I could tell, come close to it."

"One component of grief, as I know you know," Susan said, "is 'What will become of me?'"

I nodded.

"Perhaps that feeling has somewhat overshadowed her others," Susan said.

"Thank you, Dr. Silverman," I said. "Would that be narcissism?"

"Maybe," Susan said. "To make a thing for her out of his tragedy."

She drank some champagne.

"Or maybe it's a way of coping bravely with unspeakable sorrow," I said.

"Maybe," Susan said.

"Are you shrinks ever certain of anything?"

"Possibly," she said. "Have you talked to Prince's colleagues?"

"Cops have. They say there's nothing there."

"How about students?" Susan said.

"Don't think so."

"Office staff?" she said.

"I don't think so," I said.

"Both offer insights often unavailable to colleagues," Susan said.

"Maybe I'll go over there," I said. "Talk to the coeds. Coeds can't resist me."

"As long as you can resist them," Susan said.

"I value maturity," I said.

"You should," she said. "Is that stew done?"

"With stew," I said, "if you cook it right, you have a *done* window of about six hours."

"That should allow time for sex," she said.

"If we hurry," I said.

"Good. I like lovemaking on an empty stomach."

"Me, too," I said. "Or a full one. Or one partly empty. Or—"

She turned against me on the couch.

"Stop talking," she said.

And gave me a large kiss.

11

The Department of Art and Art History at Walford was located on the first floor of a brick building with Georgian pillars beside a pond. The pond looked to me as if it didn't belong there and had recently been created. But maybe I was being picky. Ponds are nice. The main office was right inside the front doorway, to the right. There were three women there. The presiding woman was tall and gray-haired, with thin lips and grim eyes. On her desk was a nameplate that said *Agnes Phelen.* Her desk was beside a door that led to the office of the department chairman. I knew that at once, because I am a trained investigator and the sign on the pebbled-glass door said *Office of the Department Chairman.* The other two women were much younger and looked more optimistic. Agnes looked at me with what appeared to be scorn, though it could have been suspicion.

"May I help you?" she said.

She didn't look as though she meant it.

"You may," I said.

She looked annoyed.

"What would you like?" she said.

"My name is Spenser," I said. "I'm a detective looking into the death of Ashton Prince."

"Dr. Prince," she said. "A terrible shame."

"What can you tell me about him?" I said.

"A fine scholar and a fine gentleman," she said.

"Anything unusual about him?" I said.

"No," she said.

From the corner of my eye I saw the two other women look at each other.

"You ladies tell me anything about Dr. Prince?"

They both shook their heads, but there was a mutual smirk hidden somewhere in the head shakes.

"He get along with everyone?" I said.

One of the younger women said, "Uh-huh."

But it didn't sound as though she meant it.

"Never any trouble."

"Of course not," Agnes said. "This is an academic office."

"Well," I said. "He had trouble with someone."

"You know who killed him?" one of the younger women said.

Agnes gave her the gimlet eye.

"You girls have work to do," Agnes said.

They both turned back to their computers, sneaking sidelong looks at each other.

"And I have work to do, too, if you'll excuse me."

"You're excused," I said. "Is there a place around here to get lunch?"

"We all use the faculty café," one of the young women said. "In the basement of Sarkassian."

"Unless you are faculty or staff," Agnes said, "I don't believe you're allowed."

"Thanks," I said.

The younger women looked at me. I winked at them and left the office.

12

I found Sarkassian Hall on a circular drive opposite the library. I went to the basement and walked into the faculty cafeteria, trying to bear myself like a man thinking deeply about John Milton. No one paid any attention to me. I could have been thinking about Sarah Palin, for all they cared. It was eleven-thirty. I got a cup of coffee and a large corn muffin and sat at an empty table where I could see the door, and waited.

I had finished my coffee and my corn muffin by the time the two young women from the art office arrived at twelve-ten. They each got a salad and carried it to a table at the other end of the cafeteria. I got up and walked over to them.

"Could I buy you lunch?" I said.

"We already paid," one of them said. "But you can sit if you want."

"Thank you," I said.

I sat.

"My name's Spenser," I said. "As you probably gathered, I'm trying to find out who killed Ashton Prince."

"We heard you in the office," one of them said. "My name's Tracy. This is Carla."

Tracy had shoulder-length dark hair and was a little heavy. Nothing a modest workout schedule wouldn't fix. Carla was slimmer, with brown hair in a ponytail. Neither one was a stunner. But neither one was beyond the pale, either.

"Agnes minding the store?" I said.

"We have lunch while she covers the office," Tracy said. "And then we cover the office while she has lunch."

"Doesn't trust either of you to do it alone?" I said.

"Big job," Carla said.

"She tries to make it a big job," Tracy said. "You know, making sure nobody uses the copy machine unless authorized. Important stuff like that."

"She hard to work for?" I said.

Tracy shrugged.

"We don't really work for her. But she's the chairman's secretary and we're just department pool workers, so it sort of works out that way."

"Actually," Carla said, "she's pathetic. You know? I mean, me and Tracy working here is just, you know, a step along the way. Pay's good, benefits are great. My husband's a carpenter in town, on his own, no benefits. Tracy's hub is working on a Ph.D. here. We got lives."

"And she's got?"

"The job," Carla said. "Period. So she makes it into a damn religion. The department is perfect. The professors walk on freaking water."

"And," Tracy said, "if she weren't ever-vigilant, it would all go to hell."

"So what didn't she tell me?" I said.

"Why do you think she didn't tell you something?" Carla said.

"I'm a trained detective," I said.

"Wowie," Tracy said.

"So tell me about Ashton Prince," I said. "The part that made you two sort of giggle at each other."

"Ash liked the ladies," Tracy said.

"Especially the young ones," Carla said.

"How young?" I said.

"Mostly younger than us," Carla said.

"Not to say he didn't give us a chance," Tracy said.

"Which you declined?" I said.

"I like my husband a lot better than I liked Ash Prince," Tracy said.

"Absolutely," Carla said.

"Students?" I said.

"You betcha," Tracy said.

"Any one in particular?"

"Changed from semester to semester," Tracy said.

"But he usually got them from his seminar," Carla said.

"He gave a seminar every semester, 'Low-Country Realists,'" Tracy said.

"Which is where he trolled for them," Carla said. "He's something of a legend among the women students."

"What happened to his seminar?" I said.

"Kids will all get the grade they had on the midterm for a final grade. Ash was a notoriously easy grader. Nobody's complaining."

"You don't happen to know who his current favorite was," I said.

"Don't have a name. But there was a blonde girl, tall, very artsy-looking in a sort of fake way," Tracy said. "You know. Long, smooth hair; high boots; too-long cashmere sweaters; pre-torn designer jeans. She spent a lot of time in his office."

"When does the seminar meet?" I said.

"Tuesdays, two to five, in the Fine Arts building," Carla said. "Room Two-fifty-six."

"Right on the tip of your tongue," I said.

"I spent most of a day trying to schedule a replacement for Ash when he got killed," she said. "It's burned into my brain."

I gave each of them my business card.

"Hey," Tracy said. "You're not a cop."

"Private," I said. "You think of anything, you could call me."

"A private eye?" Carla said. "You carry a gun?"

"I do," I said.

"You ever shoot anybody?"

"Mostly I use it to get a date," I said.

13

I went over to the campus police station and sat with the chief, a tall, pleasant-looking guy with short sandy hair and horn-rimmed glasses. His name was Crosby.

"Frank Belson said I should talk to you," he said. "I started out in a cruiser with Frank back in the days when we were two to a car, working out of the old station house in Brighton."

"Right across from Saint Elizabeth's."

"You got it," Crosby said. "Met a lotta nurses from Saint Elizabeth's in those days. Me and Frank both. We had some pretty wild times off-duty, and a few when we were on."

"What do you know about Ashton Prince?" I said.

Crosby's face got quiet, and he sucked on his cheeks for a moment.

"Belson tells me your word is good," he said.

"It is," I said.

"Belson and I grew up together in the cop business, until I took retirement after twenty, and came to work here."

"Belson's a lifer," I said.

"For sure," Crosby said. "Frank's approval carries a lot of weight with me. And we got a guy murdered here, one of ours, even though he was pretty much of a jerkoff."

"Lot of that going around in academe," I said.

"Sweet Jesus," Crosby said.

I waited. He sucked his cheeks for another moment.

"Okay," Crosby said. "What I say in this room stays in this room."

I nodded.

"Your word?"

"I'll use the information, but I won't say where I got it without your permission."

"Okay," Crosby said.

He sat back a little in his chair and put his feet up on his desk. He was wearing cordovan shoes with a high shine.

"This is an easy job," Crosby said. "Most of the time I don't even carry a piece. We make sure that everyone parks in the right place. We keep the kids from setting fire to the place while drunk. We do routine patrol."

"Keep the marauders at bay," I said.

"Something like that," Crosby said. "Now and then a rape. Now and then a robbery. But mostly it's sort of house-keeping, you know, and, ah, covering up."

"'Covering up'?"

"University dislikes scandal," Crosby said. "Made that clear when they hired me. Part of my job description is keeping a lid on anything that might harm enrollments, recruiting, or, God forbid, fund-raising and alumni support."

"How you feel about that?" I said.

Crosby smiled.

"I don't like it," he said. "But in a way it's kind of motivational. We work extra hard to prevent a crime from happening so we don't have to cover it up."

"Then along came Prince?" I said.

Crosby nodded.

"He can't stay away from the female students. You know, famous professor, handsome, good dresser in a fluty kind of way. Got that fake English accent that they used to teach movie stars in the thirties and forties. Lot of girls are happy to hook up with him. He's scored a bunch of them. But he wants to score all of them. We have complaints of sexual harassment, sexual innuendo, inappropriate touching, stalking, offering to swap grades for sex."

"And how does the university feel about that?"

"They don't like it. But he's a tenured professor and a well-known international expert on some kind of art."

"Probably low-country realism," I said.

"Sure," Crosby said. "It's how I got to know him. I was bringing him in and talking to him so often we got to know each other pretty well."

"How did he behave when you spoke of his behavior?" I said.

"He was shocked—shocked, I tell you."

"Denied it?"

"Denied it absolutely," Crosby said. "Said the girls must be either vindictive that he spurned them—his words—or they were fantasizing and allowed the fantasy to overcome them."

"All of them?"

"All," Crosby said. "He absolutely rejected every complaint. Said he had an attorney, and if we brought charges he would sue the girls, sue the university, probably sue me, for all I know."

"Do you know the name of the lawyer?"

"No, but the university counsel does."

He swung his chair sideways and picked up a phone and punched in a number.

"George," he said to the phone. "Mike Crosby. Who's the lawyer that Ashton Prince used to threaten us with?"

He waited, then nodded and wrote down a name on the pad of yellow lined paper on his desk.

"Thanks, George," he said. "No, nothing. Just sorting the case out for myself. Sure, George. Mum's the word. Thanks."

He looked at me.

"That's the motto of our department. Lot of departments have like 'to protect and serve'? We have 'Mum's the word.'"

He ripped the sheet of paper off the pad and handed it to me.

"Morton Lloyd," he said. "In Boston."

I folded it and put it in my pocket.

"So the university decided to do nothing about Prince," I said.

"No, they decided to keep it quiet," Crosby said. "That's doing something."

"In loco parentis," I said.

Crosby nodded.

"Ain't it something," he said.

"Can you do me a favor?" I said.

"Long as mum's the word," Crosby said.

I smiled.

"Prince was teaching a seminar called 'Low-Country Realists' when he was killed," I said. "A teaching assistant is finishing it up. Class meets from two to five on Tuesdays."

"You want to sign up for it?" Crosby said.

"I want a list of the students," I said.

"Sure," he said. "You got a fax?"

"Of course," I said. "I'm a high-tech sleuth."

I gave him my card.

"I'll fax it to you this afternoon," Crosby said. "Why do you want it?"

"I don't know," I said. "Just blundering around in the brush here, see what I kick up."

Crosby grinned.

"That's called police work," he said.

14

I called Rita Fiore in the morning. Rita had once been a Norfolk County prosecutor. Now she was a litigator at Cone, Oakes.

"Tell me about a lawyer named Morton Lloyd," I said.

"Mort the Tort," she said. "Got his own firm, Lloyd and Leiter, offices downtown, Milk Street, maybe. What are you looking for."

"Wish I knew," I said. "What should I know about him?"

"He's smart. He's tough. I don't think he tests out so good on ethics, but if I were going to sue somebody, Mort would be my guy. You want to sue somebody?"

"Nope. I'm just nosing around," I said.

"I hear you're involved in that art heist and murder," Rita said.

"Who says?"

"I'm sort of friendly with Kate Quaggliosi," Rita said.

"Isn't she a blabbermouth," I said.

"What are friends for?" Rita said. "She's a pretty smart cupcake."

"Smart as you?" I said.

"Of course not," Rita said. "Not as hot, either."

"Who is?" I said.

"How would you know," Rita said.

"I am a skilled observer," I said.

"You're not ready to cheat on Susan, are you?" Rita said.

"When I am, you'll be the first to know," I said.

"How encouraging," Rita said.

"I assume Lloyd charges a lot for his services," I said.

"A lot," Rita said.

"Ashton Prince, the guy that got blown up, claims that Lloyd was his attorney."

"On a professor's salary?" Rita said.

"Maybe pro bono?" I said.

"Mort doesn't do pro bono," Rita said. "You going to talk to him?"

"I suspect that he wouldn't tell me which way east was, if I went in."

"I suspect you're right," Rita said. "You want me to talk with him?"

"Yes."

"What do you want to know?"

"Anything he'll tell you. Did he have a professional relationship with Ashton Prince? If he did, what for? How was Prince planning to pay his fee? Stuff like that."

"No problem," Rita said. "Mort's always lusted for me."

"And you for him?"

"No," Rita said. "But he doesn't know that."

"Is it ethical to use sex as a tool of exploitation?"

"'Tool' may be an unfortunate choice of words," Rita said. "But the nice thing about Mort is you don't have to sweat ethics or morality with him."

"Makes it easier," I said.

"Do you want your name mentioned?"

"Not unless you think you need to, and I can't see why you would."

"Me, either," Rita said. "I assume this is pro bono."

"Not at all," I said. "I plan to reward you with a long lunch at Locke's."

"I accept," Rita said. "And afterward?"

"I'll be a perfect gentleman."

"Damn," she said.

15

Susan and Pearl were spending the weekend. Pearl was sprawled on the couch with her head hanging off, snoring faintly. I was making some green-apple fritters. Susan stood at the living-room window, looking down toward the Public Garden.

"When I took her down there this morning," Susan said, "Pearl kept snuffing around, and stopping and looking at me, and then snuffing around some more. I think she was looking for Otto."

"Love alters not when it alteration finds," I said.

"I've noticed that," Susan said. "Especially when Rita Fiore is around."

"I'm not sure that's love," I said. "And I'm not sure I'm its exclusive object."

"Probably not," Susan said. "Have you seen her lately?"

"Talked to her today on the phone."

"About the art-theft murder?"

I was peeling an apple.

"Yep. She's going to find some stuff out from a lawyer she knows," I said, "whom she says lusts after her."

"I'm sure he does," Susan said. "She's very attractive."

"She is," I said.

"Great hair," Susan said. "You don't always see a redhead with hair that good."

"That's probably not why Morton Lloyd lusts after her," I said.

Susan continued to look down toward the Public Garden.

"I'm going to take her to lunch at Locke's," I said. "As a payoff."

Susan turned and looked at me.

"I'm sure you'll have a lovely time," she said.

"I'm sure I will," I said. "Rita's a lot of fun."

"And she's so good-looking," Susan said.

"She is," I said.

Susan was quiet. I peeled my apples. Pearl snored.

"Do you think she's better-looking than *moi*?" Susan said.

What kind of idiot wouldn't know the right answer to that? But in fact I did think she was better-looking than Rita, though the gap was maybe not as wide as I would imply.

"No," I said.

"Do you think I'm better-looking than she?" Susan said.

"Absolutely," I said.

"Would you care to elaborate a bit?"

"Sure," I said.

I tossed my sliced apples in a bowl with a little lemon juice to keep them from turning brown.

"You are the best-looking woman I've ever known," I said. "Also, your hair is better than Rita's."

"Black hair is easier," she said.

I measured some flour into another bowl.

"No doubt," I said. "But it remains true. And if it didn't, if none of it were true, would it really matter? We love each other, and we're in it for the long haul."

"Yes," Susan said.

I sprinkled some nutmeg into the flour.

"So what difference does it make?" I said.

Susan nodded.

"You don't think her ass is better than mine?" Susan said.

"No one's is," I said. "And I pay close attention."

She nodded and turned back to the window. I broke a couple of eggs into my batter mix.

"What do you need to learn from this lawyer?" Susan said.

"I don't know, really. It's like what I do. I look into something and I get a name and I look into the name and it leads to another name, and I keep finding out whatever I can about whatever comes my way, and sometimes you find something that helps."

Susan left the window and came and sat on a stool at my kitchen counter. She had on tight black jeans tucked into high black boots. On top she was wearing a loose aqua silk T-shirt, narrowed at the waist by a fancy belt.

"So what have you found so far?" Susan said.

I told her what I knew. She listened with her usual luminous intensity.

"The male version of Rita Fiore," Susan said.

"How unkind," I said.

"Horny?" Susan said.

"I was thinking of something a little more technical," I said.

"Satyriasis?" Susan said.

"There you go," I said. "Is it real, or just a term, like nymphomania, which ascribes an illness to behavior we disapprove of."

"Both can be legitimate," she said. "Though talking of nymphomania is sort of incorrect these days. But both are tied to a definition which depends to some extent on the observer's view of normal and abnormal."

" 'Nothing human is foreign to me,' " I said.

She smiled.

"Thank you, Mr. Whitman," she said. "On the other hand, rape and murder are human, too."

"Okay, we'll give Walt some poetic license," I said.

"To me it's more a matter of degree, and effect."

I poured some safflower oil into my big frying pan, and let it heat.

"Like booze," I said.

"Yes," Susan said. "You like to drink. But you can choose not to. You can stop when it's appropriate. It doesn't interfere with your work, or our relationship, or anything else. But if you had to drink and couldn't stop and it was screwing up your life, and mine, then you have an illness, alcoholism, and you'd need help."

"So if I'm that way about sex, have to have it, can't restrain myself, force myself on people . . ."

"That's just you being you," Susan said.

"Wait a minute," I said.

She laughed.

"I couldn't resist," she said.

"Maybe you have an illness?" I said.

"No doubt," she said. "But your analogy is apt. If you are, so to speak, a sexual alcoholic, then you have an illness, and you need help."

"Would someone like that be likely to seek help?"

"I don't know. Most people with whatever problem don't seek shrink help. I've had very few cases of either men or women with out-of-control sexual issues."

"Would men be likely to seek help from a woman?" I said.

"They might," Susan said. "It might excite them to think of talking about it with a woman. Are you thinking Prince sought help?"

"I don't know. Certainly the college would have a shrink on retainer, wouldn't they?"

"Most colleges do," Susan said. "Why are you investigating Prince so carefully? He's the victim."

With a pair of tongs, I began to place the batter-coated apple rings into the hot oil.

"The fact that they planned ahead of time to kill him makes me wonder a little," I said.

"Because they prepared the bomb and everything?" Susan said.

"Yeah," I said. "They didn't improvise that at the spur of the moment."

"No," Susan said. "Of course."

"And," I said, "more important, he's all I've got. I don't investigate him, and I may as well be sitting on the dock of the bay."

"Yes," Susan said. "It's not so different than what I do."

I took a few fritters out of the fry pan, added a little oil, let it heat, and placed a few more rings in there.

"Why so few at a time?" Susan said. "There's room for more."

"You crowd them and they don't come out right," I said.

"I didn't know that," Susan said.

"You would if you needed to," I said.

"Would Rita?"

"Not as well as you would," I said.

"Right answer," Susan said.

"No fool I."

16

The fax from Crosby finally arrived in my office on Monday morning. There were eight names on it. Three of them were women. One of them was Melissa Minor. I sat back in my chair. Melissa Minor. Minor wasn't an exotic name. But it wasn't particularly common, either. I could not remember, in the course of my lifetime, meeting anyone named Minor. And now on the same case in a matter of days I encounter two?

I swiveled around and picked up my phone and called Crosby.

"Spenser," I said. "Thanks for the fax."

"Maybe I'll change the department motto," Crosby said. "Stay mum and be helpful?"

"Needs work," I said. "Can you get me the name of Melissa Minor's mother?"

"Who's Melissa Minor?"

"One of the students in Prince's seminar," I said.

"Oh, hell, I didn't even read the list," Crosby said. "When they sent it to me, I had my secretary fax it on over."

"Sure," I said. "Can you get me her mother's name?"

"Yeah, they'll have that." I could hear the smile in his voice. "Where they probably send the tuition bill."

"Lemme know," I said.

"Call you back," Crosby said. "This is exciting. I almost feel like a cop."

"Try to remain calm," I said.

We hung up.

While I waited, I looked out my window at the corner of Berkeley and Boylston. While I'd been spinning my wheels, we'd settled into December, and every commercial enterprise that would support a Christmas decoration had several. It hadn't snowed yet. But it was cold, and the young women who worked in the area were bundled up so that it was less fun to watch them walk by than it was in the summer. But it wasn't no fun. And though my commitment to Susan was absolute, that was no reason not to survey the landscape.

The phone rang.

"Mother's name is Winifred Minor," Crosby said. "No father listed. Mother lives in Charlestown. Employed at Shawmut Insurance on Columbus Ave."

"You know if the father's deceased?" I said.

"Don't know nothing about the father," Crosby said. "I asked about that. Told me in the admissions office that when she filled out the forms she simply drew a line in the space where it said 'father's name.'"

"What's the address?" I said.

Crosby gave it to me. I thanked him and hung up. I sat for a while, looking at nothing. Then I got up and walked around my office, which isn't really big enough for walking. I stood at my window and looked down at Berkeley Street. Then I sat down again. The more information I got, the less I understood.

"Hello," I said to no one. "Any Minotaurs in there?"

17

I was lingering as inconspicuously as I could on the second floor of the Fine Arts building, outside the room where the "Low-Country Realism" seminar was finishing up. Since I was the only person in the corridor at the moment, I was about as inconspicuous as a wolverine in a hair salon. But, master of disguise that I am, I was carrying Simon Schama's book on Rembrandt under my arm.

No one paid much attention to me as class let out. It was a no-brainer. There was only one tall blonde, and except for hair color, which is not immutable, she looked very much like her mother. She was wearing a thick white cable-knit sweater that looked a couple of sizes too big for her. Below the sweater were very tight black jeans. The jeans were tucked into high tan boots with white fur trim around the tops. If she was dressing like an artist, it was a successful artist. The boots cost more than everything I was wearing, including my gun. Over her left arm she was carrying a fleece-lined leather coat with a fleece collar. She had neither books nor a notebook. She was talking with the other two girls when I interrupted.

"Excuse me," I said. "Melissa?"

"Missy," she said, as if the correction was automatic.

"Missy Minor," I said. "Has a nice ring to it, doesn't it?"

"Who are you?" she said.

"My name is Spenser," I said. "I'm a detective."

"Is it about Dr. Prince?" Missy said.

The two girls with her were both shorter than Missy. One wore a sweatshirt with a Red Sox logo. The other had on a short plaid skirt and cowboy boots.

"Yes," I said, and turned to the two other girls. "What are your names?"

"Sandy Wilson," the one in the sweatshirt said.

"Bev DeCarlo," the other one said.

"I don't know anything," Missy said.

"Me, either," Sandy said.

"I told the other policeman I don't know anything," Bev said.

"Don't be so hard on yourselves," I said. "You had class with him for nearly a semester. I'll bet you know a lot."

"I gotta go," Missy said. "I got another class."

"At five o'clock?" I said.

"Gotta go," Missy said, and walked away.

"The other cop just came and talked to the class after Dr. Prince was killed," Bev said. "He didn't tell us anything."

"We read about it in the papers," Sandy said. "It's very awful."

"Yep," I said. "If we could talk, maybe you could help."

"Help?" Bev said.

"More I know," I said, "more chance there is I'll catch the bastards."

"We were going down to the pub," Sandy said. "You wanna come along?"

"Okay with you, Bev?" I said.

"Sure," she said. "Actually, you're kind of cute."

"Everybody tells me that," I said.

18

The pub was in the student union, off the student cafeteria. A sign at the door said *Proper ID Required for Service.* It was neat and clean, with a lot of glass and stainless steel. It didn't look like a pub. It looked like the cocktail lounge at an airport. There was music I didn't like that was playing in the room. But it was discreet enough so we could talk. Things were slow still, and the room was two-thirds empty.

Bev and I had a beer. Sandy had a glass of chardonnay.

"Thank God it's evening," Bev said.

We drank. They drank faster. They were nearly through the first drink by the time I got to my interrogation.

"Did you like Dr. Prince?" I said.

"Well, sure," Sandy said. "I mean, the poor man."

"You don't need to like him because he was killed," I said. "Did you like him when he was alive?"

They looked at each other. It was apparently a harder question than I had expected. While they looked, I got the waitress and ordered another round.

"I always had the feeling," Sandy said after the drinks came, "that he was, like, looking through my clothes."

Sandy was slight, with brown hair and glasses and nice eyes.

"Face it," Bev said. "He was a cockhound."

Bev was dark-haired and somewhat zaftig, with a slight almond shape to her eyes.

"He ever make an attempt on your virtue?" I said.

"He made an attempt on everyone's virtue," Sandy said.

"He succeed much?" I said.

"Not with me," Sandy said firmly.

I looked at Bev. She grinned at me. Both girls had emptied their glasses again. We got another round. Sometimes it went easier with booze.

After the waitress left, I said, "How about you, Bev?"

She nodded slowly.

"We had a night," she said. "He seemed like he was in a hurry."

"How so?" I said.

"It was like . . . you know, not a lot of foreplay."

"Slam, bam, thank you, ma'am," I said.

Bev laughed.

"Exactly," she said. "It was like once he got me into bed, he wanted to get it over with and move on somewhere."

"Probably the next girl," Sandy said.

Bev smiled again.

"Like I said, he's a cockhound . . . was."

"He, ah, friendly," I said, "with others in the class?"

"Others?" Sandy said. "The only other girl in class is Missy. He wasn't interested in the boys."

"Was he friendly with Missy?" I said.

"Sure," Sandy said.

I could hear the wine in her voice.

"How friendly?"

"She liked him," Bev said.

"She was sort of his girlfriend, I think," Sandy said.

"Doesn't seem the girlfriend type," I said.

Sandy shrugged.

"She never said much," Sandy said. "But I know she was with him a lot."

"You didn't like him," I said to Sandy.

"I thought he was a creepy old guy. I didn't want to see him with his clothes off. . . ." She made a face.

"But you liked him," I said to Bev.

I had no idea where I was going. I just wanted to keep them talking and see if anything popped out.

"Not really," Bev said. "But I kinda liked the idea of bopping a professor, you know? Only once, though."

"Ever meet his wife?" I said.

They both shook their heads.

"I didn't know he had one," Bev said.

"I guess neither did he," Sandy said.

"Would it have mattered?" I said to Bev.

"Hell, no," Bev said. "That's between him and her. Not up to me to, you know, keep him faithful to his wife."

"True," I said.

We lasted another hour. I didn't learn anything else. But they had gotten drunk enough so I wouldn't have had much faith in anything they told me, anyway. I stood.

"Good night, ladies," I said.

"How 'bout you," Bev said. "You married?"

"Kind of," I said.

"You cheat?" Bev said.

"No," I said.

"Really?" Bev said.

"Really," I said. "But thanks for asking."

19

got Missy Minor's campus address from Crosby, and in the mid-morning I fell into step with her when she came out.

"You're that detective," she said.

"Spenser's the name," I said. "Law and order's the game."

"I told you yesterday that I don't know anything about Dr. Prince, except that he was an okay teacher and an easy grader."

"I heard you were his girlfriend," I said.

She was silent for a beat.

Then she said, "That's crazy. Where'd you hear that."

"I'm a detective, "I said. "I have my sources."

"Speaking of which," she said, "let me see your badge."

I took a business card from my pocket and handed it to her.

"Private," I said. "Working with the police."

"'Private'?" she said, looking at my card. "A private detective? I don't have to talk with you."

"But why wouldn't you?" I said. "I'm a lot of fun."

"Yeah," she said. "I can see that."

"Plus," I said, "we have a connection."

"What?" she said.

"I know your mother," I said.

Again, a short silence.

Then she said, "You know Winifred?"

"I do," I said.

"You been talking to her about me and Dr. Prince?"

"No," I said. "If I did, what would I say?"

"My mother's a worrier," Missy said. "She heard any of your bullshit theory about me being his girlfriend, she'd go crazy."

"Even though there's no truth to it."

"She's a worrier," Missy said.

"How about your father?" I said.

"Don't have one," Missy said.

"Ever?"

She shook her head.

"I don't want to discuss it," she said.

"Did you have any sort of relationship with Ashton Prince?" I said.

She shook her head again.

"Why do you suppose people had the idea that you did?" I said.

"You're the detective," she said. "You figure it out."

"He hit on you?"

"He was my professor," she said. "That's all. I don't see why you're harassing me like this. It's not my fault I was in his class, and it's not my fault somebody blew him up with his damn painting."

The other girls hadn't mentioned the painting. It wasn't secret. But you needed to be interested to remember that the infernal device had been the painting, or something everyone thought was the painting.

"I'm going to be late," Missy said. "I wish you wouldn't bother me about this anymore."

"I'm sure I won't need to," I said.

She scooted off into the science building. I watched her go. *Liar, liar, pants on fire.*

20

I took Winifred Minor to lunch at Grill 23, which was handily equidistant between her office and mine. We sat at the bar. It was kind of early in the day for the warming pleasures of alcohol, so I ordered iced tea. She ordered a glass of chardonnay. "So," I said, and raised my glass of tea. "Here's looking at you, kid."

"You can't toast wine with tea," she said.

"You can't?"

"No," she said seriously. "It's bad luck."

"I didn't know that," I said. "Thank God you warned me in time."

She smiled. But she didn't pick up her glass until I put mine down. Then she raised hers for a sip.

"Missy Minor?" I said.

She finished her sip and put her glass carefully back down on the bar.

"What about Missy Minor?" she said.

"Your daughter?"

"Yes."

"Attractive girl," I said.

"You've spoken with her?"

"Yes."

"Why?" Winifred said.

"You know how this kind of thing works," I said. "You got nothing, so you start snooping around, looking for a loose end to tug on."

"And you decided my daughter was such?" Winifred said.

"I went over to Walford, where Prince taught, and talked with everyone I could find. Your daughter was one of them."

"And you've singled her out?" Winifred said.

"Of course," I said. "I find a woman in Prince's class whose mother is handling the insurance claims on the crime in which Prince was killed?"

"There's no connection," Winifred said.

"I'm sure there isn't," I said. "But it's too big a coincidence to let it slide."

"Coincidences happen," she said.

I had ordered a small shellfish sampler for lunch. She was having Caesar salad.

"They do," I said.

I put some red sauce on a littleneck clam, and ate. She messed around with her fork in her salad bowl. But she didn't put any food in her mouth.

"And I'd have been more willing to accept that," I said, "if you had mentioned to me that there was a daughter."

"I didn't consider it germane," Winifred said. "I was unaware that she knew Prince."

"Was she an art major?"

"Yes."

"At Walford?"

"Yes, of course," she said. "You know that."

"How long were you with the Bureau?" I said.

"Fifteen years."

I ate a shrimp. She appeared to be counting the anchovies in her salad. The bar was partly full. Mostly people having lunch but a sprinkling of thank-God-it's-noontime people. Men, mostly, who worked in the big insurance companies. No wonder they drank.

"And you didn't think someone would discover this coincidence?"

"That's all it is," she said.

"I hate coincidences," I said. "They don't do anything for anybody, and they muddy up the water to beat hell."

She studied her anchovies some more.

"Who's her father?" I said.

Winifred shook her head silently.

"I'm almost sure there has to be one," I said.

"He died," Winifred said.

"Sorry to hear that," I said. "Is it recent?"

"He died a long time ago."

"What was his name?" I said.

She shook her head again.

"How come Missy won't talk about him, either?"

Winifred took in a long, slow breath. It sounded a little shaky. Then she stood.

"Thanks for lunch," she said, and left me alone with her anchovies.

Spenser, master inquisitor.

21

The special agent in charge of the Boston FBI office was a guy named Epstein who looked less dangerous than a chickadee, and had killed, to my knowledge, two men, both of whom had probably made the same misjudgment. I had coffee with him in a joint on Cambridge Street.

"Winifred Minor," he said. "Why do you ask?"

"She used to be FBI," I said.

"Yep, but why do you ask?"

"You know I'm involved with that art theft where the guy got blown up," I said.

"Ashton Prince," Epstein said. "Hermenszoon painting."

"Wow," I said. "Sees all, knows all."

"Only a matter of time," Epstein said, "before I'm director."

"No dresses," I said.

"Prude," Epstein said. "What's your interest in Winifred Minor?"

There was a platter of crullers under a glass cover on the counter. I eyed them.

"She's a claims adjuster now," I said. "For a big insurance company."

"Shawmut," Epstein said.

"You keep track," I said.

"I do," Epstein said.

"They insured the painting," I said.

"And the claim is her case," Epstein said.

"And her daughter was a student of Prince's, and probably they had a relationship."

"Which is to say he was fucking her?" Epstein said.

"You civil servants speak so elegantly," I said. "But yes. I believe he was."

"Could all mean nothing," he said.

"Could," I said.

"But it's probably more productive to think it means something," Epstein said.

"You know who the father is, or was?" I said.

"Didn't know Winifred was married," Epstein said.

"Don't know that she was."

Epstein nodded.

"How old's the kid," he said.

"Nineteen, twenty," I said.

"So Winifred was still with the Bureau," Epstein said, "when the kid was born."

I nodded. Epstein drank some of his coffee. I studied the plate of crullers some more.

"You ask either of them about the father?" Epstein said.

"I did," I said.

"And?"

"They won't talk about him," I said.

"When the baby was born she probably used her health insurance," Epstein said. "Bureau will have a record. I'll see what I can find out. What's the kid's name?"

"Melissa Minor," I said. "Goes by Missy."

Epstein nodded. He didn't write it down. He rarely wrote things down. I sometimes thought he remembered everything he'd ever heard.

"Why are you interested in the father?"

"Seems odd they won't talk about him," I said.

Epstein nodded.

"Anything's better than nothing," Epstein said.

"But harder to come by," I said. "You know Winifred Minor?"

"Casually," Epstein said. "Bureau regarded her as a good agent, maybe a little gung ho."

"Aggressive?"

"Yep. Probably proving something 'cause she was a female agent," Epstein said.

"She know anything about explosives?"

Epstein shrugged.

"No reason she should," he said. "I don't."

"I thought special agents in charge knew everything," I said.

"They do," Epstein said. "I was just being modest."

22

I t had snowed in the night, and the world looked very clean, which I knew it not to be. But illusion is nice sometimes.

Susan was at a conference in Fitchburg, so Pearl was spending the day with me. We got to work a little before nine, and Pearl scooted into the office across the hall from mine to see Lila, the receptionist. Lila gave her a cookie, which she always did when Pearl came to visit, which may have been why Pearl was always eager to see her.

"Hi, big boy," Lila yelled to me.

I stopped and stuck my head in her doorway.

I said, "How's the modeling career, Toots?"

"I think I got a photo gig," she said. "Car dealer on the north shore."

"I hope you don't get too successful," I said. "I like seeing you across the hall."

Pearl was sitting still and focused, studying the drawer in Lila's desk where she knew the cookies were kept, on the off chance that today, for the only time, Lila would give her another one. But Lila and I had agreed that since Pearl was insatiable, and you'd have to say no eventually, you might as well say no after one cookie.

"Sooner or later," Lila said, "we'll have to stop meeting like this."

I nodded sadly and jerked my head at Pearl. We went across the hall to my office. As I took out my keys, Pearl stopped stock-still and began to growl. It wasn't her usual sort of rambunctious there's-a-dog-I-don't-know-passing-the-house growl. This was primordial. A low, steady sound that seemed to pulsate. I stared at her. The hair was up along her spine. Her nose was pressed against the crack where the closed door met the jamb. The growl was unvarying. It was as if she didn't need to breathe. There was a hint of snowmelt on the floor. I looked down the hall. It was dry, except at Lila's office, where I'd left some wet footprints. I stepped to the side, away from the door, and took Pearl with me.

Pearl was idiosyncratic. She could be growling at the doorknob. But the growl was so malevolent. I reached silently over and tried the doorknob. The door was locked. I leaned my head around the jamb and put my ear to the door. I heard nothing. Maybe Pearl was wrong, though she was certainly insistent. And someone had left a trace of melted snow outside my door. And I was working on a case involving people who had blown someone into small pieces.

I took Pearl by the collar and led her back into Lila's office.

"Your door lock?" I said.

"Sure," she said.

"Okay, give her another cookie while I go out. Then lock the door behind me and keep her here while I do a little business."

"What's going on?" Lila said.

"Official detective business," I said.

"Yeah?"

"If anything unusual happens in the hallway or my office, keep your door locked and call nine-one-one."

"'Unusual'?"

"Yeah."

"Unusual, like what?" she said.

"Oh," I said. "The usual, you know. Gunfire, that kind of stuff."

"Fucking gunfire?" she said.

"Just giving you a hypothetical example," I said.

"You mean, like, I'm in danger?"

"Only if you flash that smile," I said.

"I'm serious," she said.

"No one is interested in you, except, of course, me," I said. "Sit tight and you're fine."

"Me and Pearl," she said.

I nodded. I was watching my office door as we talked. I didn't want to take my gun out, thus causing Lila to freak. But I let my hand stay close to my hip.

"What do I tell my employers?" she said. "If any of them come in."

"Tell them you're doing me a favor," I said.

"Most of them don't like you," she said.

"Oh, of course they do," I said. "How could they not?"

"And they pay my salary," she said.

"But do they feel about you the way I do?" I said.

"Probably," she said. "But nobody's due in today until late afternoon, anyway."

"I owe you," I said.

"You certainly do," Lila said.

"Lock the door," I said.

23

My office was on the second floor, with windows that opened on Berkeley Street. I went out into the hall and down the back stairs to the alley, where my car was parked illegally. The snow was still drifting down halfheartedly. I got a pair of binoculars from the car and ducked with my head down across Berkeley Street in the middle of the block, and got glared at. If there was somebody in my office, they would be watching the door, not looking at the street.

I went into the Schwartz Building across the street from my office and up to the second floor. It was the office where, when the building was in another incarnation, a dark-haired art director with great hips had often been visible from my office, bending over her board. I slid behind a counter, stood at the window, and adjusted the binoculars.

A clerk said, "Excuse me, sir. May I help you with something?"

"*Shhh,*" I said. "Surveillance."

He apparently didn't know what to say about that, so he stood and stared at me. With the binoculars I brought my office into focus. There were two of them. One sitting behind my desk with an Uzi-like automatic weapon, maybe a Colt M4. The other guy stood to the right of my door, so that he'd be behind the door when it opened. He had a handgun. Neither of them moved around any. As far as I could see from where I was, neither of them said anything.

I lowered the binoculars and looked at the clerk, who was still staring at me.

"Thanks," I said, and left.

I went back downstairs and out, and crossed Berkeley at the corner, with the light. I hated being glared at. In the alley, I took off my coat and put it on the backseat, along with the binoculars. Then I sat in my car, took out my gun, and made sure there was a round in the chamber. I got an extra magazine from the glove compartment and slipped it into my hip pocket. Then I cocked the gun and got out and went back up to my floor.

Lila's door was still closed. I stood against the wall to the right of my door and reached out and unlocked it. Nothing happened. I took the key from the lock, put it in my pocket. Then I knelt down and pushed the door open. I was out of the line of fire, low against the wall of the corridor.

Nothing happened.

I waited.

Time was on my side. The longer they sat and stared at the silent, empty doorway, the more it would be on my side. They didn't know how many I was. They didn't know which side of the doorway I was on. Or how close. If I were them I'd come out together, shooting in both directions as I came. I backed a little down the corridor and lay flat on the floor with my gun ready. It was a new gun, an S&W .40-caliber semiautomatic. There were eleven rounds in the magazine and one in the chamber. If that wasn't enough, I probably wasn't, either.

Most of the people on my floor were in sales. And except for Lila, who served as a communal secretary, there was rarely anyone around during the day. No one moved in the hall. Nothing happened at my office door. I was listening so hard that my breath seemed loud. I moved my shoulders a little, trying to keep them loose. I inhaled gently, trying to be silent.

They came out shooting. The Uzi sprayed the corridor away from me. The handgun guy fired several slugs over my head before I shot him. The man with the Uzi spun toward me, and I shot him, too. They both went down. The man with the handgun never moved. The guy with the Uzi spasmed maybe twice and then lay still. I stayed prone on the hall floor with my gun still aimed, taking in air. Then I stood and walked over and looked at them. They were dead. I uncocked my new gun and holstered it, and heaved in some more air.

Lila had called 911. I could hear the distant sirens rolling down Boylston Street.

24

Pearl and I spent pretty much the rest of the day in close contact with the Boston Police Department. First came the prowl-car guys. Then the precinct detectives, and the crime scene people. About an hour after it started, Belson came in and looked at me and shook his head.

"Wyatt Fucking Earp," he said.

I shrugged.

Belson went and talked with a crime scene investigator. Then he went over to the couch and scratched Pearl's right ear. Her short tail thumped against the cushion.

"She been out?" he said.

"Lila across the hall," I said. "Took her out about a half-hour ago."

"Okay," Belson said. "Then let's you and me gather at your desk and chat."

One of the precinct detectives said, "I've questioned him, Frank. Want me to bring you up to speed?"

"No," Belson said.

I sat at my desk. Belson pulled a chair up and sat across the desk from me.

"Crime scene guy tells me one round each. Middle of the chest both times."

I nodded again.

"Annie Fucking Oakley," Belson said. "Talk to me."

"You know about the painting got stolen?" I said. "And the guy got blown up out on Route Two trying to get it back?"

"The guy you were bodyguarding?"

"Yep."

"Nice," Belson said. "Assume I don't."

"Okay," I said.

I told my story.

As I told it, Belson sat perfectly still and listened. Like Epstein, he didn't take notes. He rarely did. But two years later, he'd be able to give you what I'd said verbatim. Cops.

When I finished, he said, "Dog saved your ass."

I nodded.

"She did."

"You figure it's connected to the art theft and the murder?"

"Don't you?" I said.

Belson shrugged.

"You've annoyed a lot of people in the last twenty years," he said.

"Why limit it?" I said.

"You're right, you been good at it all your life."

"Everybody gotta be good at something," I said.

"But," Belson said, "it don't do us much good picking names of people might want you dead."

"Too many," I said.

"So," Belson said, "assume it's connected. Why now?"

"Don't know," I said. "I been poking around at it since it happened. I must have poked something live."

"Where you been poking recently," Belson said.

"Walford University. Winifred Minor. Her daughter. Couple of her daughter's classmates."

"Most recent?"

"Missy and Winifred Minor," I said.

"Missy Minor," Belson said.

"Cute name," I said.

"Cute," Belson said. "You know either of the stiffs?"

"No," I said.

"We'll see what we can find out," Belson said.

"Lemme know," I said.

"Might," Belson said. "You turned your piece over to the crime scene people?"

"Yep."

"You got another one?" Belson said. "People trying to kill you and all."

I reached into my desk drawer and took out a .38 Chief's Special.

"Loaded," Belson said. "No trigger lock."

"Got a nice holster," I said.

"Okay," Belson said. "In that case, I won't run you in."

"Stern," I said. "But compassionate."

"And if they succeed in killing you next try," Belson said, "I'll try to catch them."

"That's encouraging," I said.

25

I was halving oranges and squeezing the juice into a glass in my kitchen when Susan appeared, fresh from the shower and the makeup mirror. I took a deep breath. Whenever I saw her I took a deep breath. It was more dignified than yelling "Jehoshaphat!"

"Isn't that a lot of trouble?" Susan said. "I like the stuff in a carton fine."

"That's pasteurized," I said. "I want the authentic experience. Unprocessed. Nothing between me and the orange, you know? *Mano a orange-o!*"

I gave her the glass and squeezed some for myself.

"You are, as they say in psychotherapeutic circles, a weird dude," Susan said.

"And yet you love me," I said.

"I know."

"It's all about the sex," I said. "Isn't it."

"Not all," Susan said. "You cook a nice breakfast, too."

She had on tight black jeans tucked into high cavalier boots, the kind where the top folds over. Her open-collared shirt was white, and over it she wore a small black sweater vest. It set off her black hair and big, dark eyes. She probably knew that.

"Good sex and a nice breakfast," I said. "An unbeatable combination."

Susan smiled.

"I don't recall anyone using the word 'good,'" she said.

"Seems to me," I said, "you were singing different lyrics an hour ago."

She actually flushed a little bit.

"Don't be coarse," she said.

"Not even in self-defense?" I said.

She grinned at me.

"Well, maybe," she said. "We were quite lively. Weren't we."

"With good reason," I said.

I finished my orange juice and poured us both some coffee. Susan wasn't anywhere near finishing her orange juice. But she might never finish it. Over the years I'd learned to proceed and let her sort it out.

Pearl was asleep on her back on the couch, with her head lolling off. She was waiting, I knew, for actual food to be prepared and served, at which time she'd get off the couch and come over and haunt us.

"I have a question," Susan said. "And a comment."

"Is this one of those questions where you also know the answer, but you'd like to hear what I have to say?"

"Yes," Susan said. "But first the comment."

"Okay."

"It was very clever of you to turn the situation around the way you did."

"You mean opening the door and sitting tight?"

"Yes. Up to that point, they had the power. They were waiting to ambush you. When you pushed the door open, you took the power from them. Now you were waiting to ambush them."

"Astounding, isn't it," I said.

"Do you think of these things in the moment?" Susan said. "Or do you keep a little list?"

"Like a quarterback with the plays on his wristband," I said.

"Whatever that means," Susan said.

"A sports metaphor," I said. "Mostly I react. But in fact, in this case, I had done it before. I used that ploy a long time ago, in London. It sort of came back to me when Pearl gave me the heads-up."

"Why do you suppose she did that?" Susan said.

"She loves me?"

"She and I both," Susan said. "But I'm serious. What

made her growl like that? You say you've never heard her make that sound before."

"No. It did not sound like her."

"So why did she?"

"A smell in the room that she hadn't encountered?"

"There must be a hundred smells," Susan said. "Cleaning people. Clients. Why this smell?"

"I don't know."

We were quiet. Pearl shifted slightly into an even more comfortable position.

"I've had dogs nearly all my life," I said. "And most of them have been German shorthaired pointers named Pearl. I try not to romanticize them. But it is very clear to me that more goes on in there than we understand."

Susan nodded.

"You think she somehow knew something was bad?" Susan said.

"Very little is known about dogs," I said.

Susan nodded and looked at Pearl.

"Well, whatever motivated her," Susan said, "good dog!"

Pearl opened her eyes and looked at Susan upside down, saw that nothing more consequential was coming her way, and closed her eyes again.

"There was also a question?" I said.

Susan emptied a packet of Splenda into her coffee and stirred it carefully.

"When Pearl warned you," she said, "and you went across

the street and looked, and saw those two men waiting for you in your office . . ."

"Yeah?"

"Why didn't you just call the police?"

" 'Call the police,' " I said.

"Yes."

I drank some coffee. Susan waited.

"I never thought of it," I said.

"Literally?"

"Literally," I said.

She nodded slowly.

"And if you had thought of it," she said, "you wouldn't have done it, anyway, would you."

"No," I said.

"Because you clean things up yourself."

"Yes."

"Still your father's son," Susan said.

"And my uncles'," I said.

She nodded.

"Still chasing the bear," she said.

"You knew the answer before you asked the question," I said.

"But I kind of wondered if you did," she said.

"You know where I came from," I said. "And you know what I do, and if I'm going to continue to do it, I can't be someone who calls the cops when there's trouble."

"Because it's bad for business?" Susan said.

"It is bad for business, and that's a perfectly rational answer, but it's not quite why," I said.

"Because it's bad for you," Susan said.

"Bingo," I said.

"To do what you do, you have to know you can take care of business yourself," Susan said.

"Yes."

"You can get help from friends . . . Hawk, for instance," Susan said. "But you're still in it. And you're in charge."

"More or less."

"You call the cops," Susan said, "and you are expected to step aside and let them handle things."

"More than expected," I said.

"You're a professional tough guy," Susan said. "And professional tough guys don't hand off."

"Wow," I said. "A sports metaphor."

"I try," Susan said. "I want to be just like you."

"I'd hate like hell to be sleeping with someone just like me," I said.

"Funny thing," Susan said. "I've never minded."

"A puzzle," I said.

"Yes," Susan said. "But there it is."

Susan's juice glass was still nearly full. She ignored it and drank some coffee.

"It meant you had to kill two men," she said. "How does that feel."

"They would have killed me," I said.

"Yes, they would have," Susan said. "But how do you feel?"

"Several ways. I won; they lost."

"And?" she said.

"Glad they didn't kill me."

"Me, too," she said.

"And I do not like killing people," I said.

"But you do it," she said.

"And will again," I said. "But I do not like it."

"You could get out of this business," Susan said.

"I could," I said.

"But you won't," she said.

"No," I said.

"Because this is what you are and who you are," she said. "And if you quit, you would like that even less."

"I'd still be with you," I said.

"I wouldn't be enough," she said.

"If you asked me to change," I said, "I'd change."

"I'll never ask you," she said.

"You'd be enough."

"We're each enough for you," she said. "The rest is speculation."

"You're a pretty smart broad," I said.

"I know," Susan said. "You're a pretty interesting guy."

"I know," I said.

"Maybe we are about more than good sex and a fine breakfast," Susan said.

"Maybe we are the two most interesting people in the world," I said.

"Probably," she said.

26

I sat at my desk with a cup of coffee and a lined yellow pad. I was making a list of what I knew and questions I had about the death of Ashton Prince. I always liked making lists. It gave me the illusion of control.

There was certainly some kind of connection among Prince and Missy Minor and, presumably, Winifred Minor. And obviously one between Prince and the museum. There was almost certainly a connection between Prince and the robbers that I didn't see. There was no reason for them to show up for the ransom exchange already prepared to kill him, unless there was more going on than was so far evident. And somewhere along the way, as I wandered through the case, I had done something to make them want to kill me.

We had a few leads: the two shooters now in the forensics lab, and the speculative relationship between Missy Minor and Ashton Prince. I wrote those down. I needed to learn more about Prince and the Minor women. I wrote that down. Digging into Prince would mean talking again with his wife. My heart sank. But I wrote it down. Detective work is not always pretty.

My office door opened. I put my hand on the .357 Mag I kept in my open top right-hand drawer.

Martin Quirk came in.

"Don't shoot," he said. "I'm an officer of the law."

"Okay," I said, and took my hand off the gun.

Quirk tossed a manila envelope on my desk, poured himself a cup of coffee from the coffeemaker on top of my file cabinet, and took it to one of my client chairs, where he sat down and took a sip.

"Whaddya doing?" he said.

"Making a list," I said.

"Things to do with the Prince killing?"

"Yep."

"Makes you feel like you know what to do," Quirk said. "Don't it."

"It's a very orderly list," I said.

"Got any information in the list?" Quirk said.

"No," I said.

"But it makes you feel like you're making progress," Quirk said.

"Exactly."

"Copy of the forensics on the two guys you iced," he said. "Take a look, tell me what you think."

I opened the envelope and browsed the report. Much of it I didn't understand.

"You understand all this stuff?" I said.

"Some of it," Quirk said.

I read on. Quirk rose and got more coffee. When I finished reading, I put the report back in the envelope and got up and poured myself some coffee and sat back down and put my feet on the desk.

"No ID," I said.

"Neither one," Quirk said.

"One guy was wearing shoes made in Holland," I said.

"That are not exported," Quirk said.

"So maybe he's Dutch."

"Maybe," Quirk said.

"Both of them are circumcised," I said.

"So maybe they're Jewish," Quirk said.

"Lotta goyim are circumcised," I said.

"Hell," Quirk said. "I'm circumcised."

"I'm not sure I wanted to know that," I said.

"Irish Catholic mother," Quirk said. "I think she was hoping they'd take the whole thing."

I grinned.

"And both these guys got a number tattooed on their forearm."

"Death camp tattoo," Quirk said. "From Auschwitz. Only camp that did it."

"But it's the same number," I said. "On both of them."

"I know."

"And," I said, "neither one of these guys was anywhere near old enough to have been in Auschwitz."

"Both appear to be in their thirties."

"So they were born, like, thirty-five years after the Holocaust," I said.

"Correct," Quirk said.

"Maybe it's a prison tattoo," I said.

"A letter and five numbers?" Quirk said. "And it wasn't crude. It was professionally done."

"Maybe it's not a prison tattoo," I said.

"It's not," Quirk said.

We were quiet.

"How 'bout an homage," I said.

"You mean like in memory of somebody who actually was in Auschwitz?" Quirk said.

"Yeah."

"Possible," Quirk said.

"If it is, there may be an actual name attached to that number," I said.

"The death camps were liberated more than sixty-four years ago," Quirk said.

"Nazis woulda kept good records," I said.

"You think the efficient cocksuckers kept a record of the numbers and the names?" Quirk said. "And saved them?"

"You know what they were like," I said.

Quirk nodded.

"Okay," Quirk said. "They kept records."

"Yes," I said.

"So where do we find them?"

"I don't know," I said.

27

I met Rosalind Wellington outside of a poetry-writing class at the Cambridge Center for Adult Education on Brattle Street.

"Remember me?" I said.

"You're that man who was with my late husband when he died," she said.

"Spenser," I said.

"Yes," she said. "I remember you."

"May I buy you a drink?" I said.

She paused for a moment and then nodded.

"Why?" she said.

"See how you are, talk about your husband," I said.

"I guess we could go to the Harvest, next door," she said.

We sat at the bar. The Harvest was a bit elegant for the likes of me. I was probably the only guy in the place wearing a gun. I asked for beer. Rosalind ordered Pernod on the rocks. When it came, she took a considerable swallow of it.

"So how are you?" I said.

"Life is for the living," she said. "I've never been one to indulge the past."

I nodded.

"So you're okay," I said.

"Loss is the price we pay for progress," she said. "Only as we leave things behind do we move forward."

"Oh, absolutely," I said. "I'm glad you are able to be so positive."

She had cleaned up her Pernod, and I nodded at the bartender to refill.

"Life is neutral," she said. "We can choose to make it positive or negative."

"Of course," I said. "That's very insightful."

"I'm a poet," she said. "Life is my subject."

"And you've chosen to make it positive."

"I choose every day," she said.

Her second Pernod arrived. She seemed positive about that, too.

"Was your husband as, what, philosophical as you are?"

She sucked in a little Pernod.

"My husband was greedy," she said. "And self-serving and sexually addicted and very concerned with what others thought."

"Bad combination for a philosopher," I said.

"Covert and driven," she said.

" 'Covert'?" I said.

She smiled sadly and swallowed some Pernod.

" 'A life of quiet desperation,' " she said. "To borrow from Emerson."

I was pretty sure she was borrowing from Thoreau, but I felt my cause would be better served by not mentioning that.

"How's your poem coming?" I said.

"I'm always working on poetry," she said.

"I was thinking of the one you were going to write about your husband's death."

"It is still in the formative stage, but I know it will be free verse," she said. "A long free-verse narrative of the soul's journey through sorrow."

"I look forward to reading it," I said.

"My husband is so difficult to render artistically," she said.

"I'll bet he is," I said. "Tell me about him."

She fortified herself for the task by draining her second Pernod. I nodded again at the bartender. He brought her a fresh drink, and she nodded her thanks imperiously. I'd noticed that certain lushes get imperious after a couple of pops, trying to prove, I suppose, that they aren't lushes.

"He was . . . He was a tapestry of pretense. Nothing about him was real. A . . . a pastiche of deceit."

"You love him?" I said.

"I thought I did. What I loved was the mask, the costume of respectability he wore to cover himself."

"I'm fascinated," I said. "Tell me about that."

She snorted, albeit imperiously.

"Prince wasn't even his name," she said.

"What was it?" I said.

"Prinz," she said. "Ascher Prinz. He was Jewish."

"Oy," I said.

She paid no attention. I didn't feel bad about that. I was pretty sure she paid no attention to anyone.

"He was ashamed of being Jewish," she said. "He never spoke of it."

"Do you know why?" I said.

"No, I don't," she said. "For me, all ethnicity is an enriching source of authenticity, without which one can hardly be a poet."

"Did he want to be a poet?" I said.

She looked startled.

"Excuse me?" she said.

"Did Ashton want to be a poet?" I said.

"God, no," she said. "Why would you think that?"

"Just a random thought," I said.

"There was no poetry in him," she said.

"Was there something in him?"

"You mean artistically?" she said.

I could see that she was trying to nurse her current Pernod, and it was stressing her.

"Artistically, professionally, intellectually, romantically, whatever," I said.

"I . . . I really can't say."

I nodded.

"When did his family come to this country?" I said.

"Ashton's?"

"Uh-huh."

"I don't really know that, either," she said, and gestured to the bartender. "I do know that his father was in a concentration camp. So it would be after World War Two, I guess."

"You know which camp?" I said.

The Pernod came. She drank some. I could almost see her tension loosen.

"Oh, I don't know. He never talked about it, and they all sound the same to me, anyway."

"You poets are so sensitive," I said.

"What?"

"Just being frivolous," I said.

"Oh," she said.

I could see that she was losing focus.

"Tell me about his, ah, sexual addiction," I said.

She sort of grunted.

"I'll tell you one thing," she said. "He wasn't addicted to me."

"Hard to imagine," I said. "Who was he addicted to?"

"I couldn't keep track," she said. "He liked college girls, I think."

"Well, he was in the right place," I said. "Do you know any names?"

"God, no. You think I cared? You think I kept track? He was just another prancing, leering goat, and the only people who could possibly have been interested in him were silly girls."

"Does the name Missy Minor mean anything to you?"

"Sounds like a silly girl to me," Rosalind said.

Her *s*'s were starting to get a little slushy.

"But you don't recognize the name?" I said.

"Silly stupid fucking girls," Rosalind said.

The window had closed. I nodded. Then I picked up the check from where the bartender had put it, and took out money and paid.

"Could I take you home?" I said.

She was staring into her Pernod glass.

"And come in?" she said.

"Just take you home," I said.

"Course not," she said. "So you just go ahead. Go ahead. I'm going to stay here and have one more . . . for the road."

"Well," I said. "Thanks for talking with me."

"Yeah," she said. "You just go ahead."

Which I did.

28

I sat with Healy and Kate Quaggliosi in a small meeting room at the Middlesex DA's office in Woburn. Kate was wearing a tailored gray suit and a white shirt with a little black lady tie at half-mast.

"You dress good for a prosecutor," I said.

"My husband's in private practice," she said.

"Money well spent," I said.

She looked at Healy.

"How about you, Captain," she said. "You think I look good?"

"Cat's ass," Healy said.

She smiled.

"Gee, thanks," she said. "Here's what we've got on the victim. Ashton Prince . . ."

I put my hand up.

"You wish to speak?" she said.

"Real name is Ascher Prinz," I said. "According to his wife, he changed it because he was ashamed of being Jewish."

"'Ashamed'?" she said.

"That's what Rosalind told me," I said.

"Rosalind," Kate said.

"I had a drink with her yesterday," I said.

"Well, aren't you just slick," Kate said.

"I've got an advantage," I said. "I'm allowed to get them drunk."

"Was that hard to do?" Kate said.

"Would have been hard not to," I said.

"Anything else you want to share," Kate said.

"His father was in a concentration camp," I said.

"Which one?" Healy said.

"She doesn't remember," I said. "They all sound the same to her."

"Jesus," Healy said.

"Should I know something that I don't know now?" Kate said.

"Last week a couple of fellas set up to ambush Spenser when he came into his office. They each had the same death camp number tattooed on their arm."

"They were that old?"

"No," I said.

"So . . . where are they now?"

"Dead," Healy said. "They were overmatched."

"'Overmatched'?" Kate said, and looked at me. "You killed them?"

"I did," I said.

Kate stared at me.

"I'll be damned," she said.

"Tough, but oh so gentle," I said.

"And you think it's connected to our case?" Kate said.

"I do," I said.

She looked at Healy.

"Captain?" she said.

"We can't assume that it's not," Healy said.

"No," Kate said. "Tell me what you know."

We told her.

"Who's working it from Boston," she said.

"Frank Belson," I said.

"I know Belson," she said.

"Everybody should," I said.

"Anybody chasing down those serial numbers?" Kate said.

"Boston Homicide," I said.

"Us, too," Healy said.

"Any luck?" Kate said.

"Not so far," Healy said.

She looked at me.

"Haven't heard," I said.

"You think it's possible that there are still records?"

"They'd have kept records," I said.

"I'll see what this office can do," she said. "Any ID on the two shooters?"

"Nope," Healy said. "They're not in the system. One of them had shoes made in Holland. The Uzi was Israeli."

"That's what you have?"

"That's what Boston was able to give us," Healy said.

"You have a theory as to what triggered it?" Kate said to me.

"Last two people I talked with before they came after me were the Minor women. Missy and Winifred."

"So they might be worth our attention," Kate said.

"Might," I said.

"We've pretty well emptied it out for you," Healy said. "You got anything we don't know?"

"Sure, but it's not worth much," Kate said. "Parents' names, birthplace, education, career history. That kind of crap."

"Can we have it?" I said.

"Sure," she said.

She pushed a couple of blue folders toward us.

"Enjoy," she said.

29

I was alone in my apartment. The door was locked. It was very quiet. I was lying on the bed, sipping some Black Bush on the rocks and reading the files on Ashton Prince that Kate Quaggliosi had given me. The file was boring. But I loved the silence.

Ashton Prince had been born forty-eight years ago in Queens, New York, and attended public school there. He had majored in art at Colby College in Waterville, Maine, and graduated in 1982. He'd gone on to acquire a Ph.D. in art history from Boston University. No mention of his parents. No mention of Ascher Prinz. He'd been a teaching fellow for a couple of years at BU while he was getting his degree. He taught art history for a couple of years at Bridgewater State College before he moved on to Walford as an assistant professor. He settled in at Walford. His specialty was seventeenth-century low-country realism, and he had written some essays for academic journals, and a book about the Nazi confiscation of art during World War Two. The book was published by Taft University Press and was titled *Aesthetics and Greed in the Second Great War.* He had spent a sabbatical year in Amsterdam. He was a tenured full professor when he died. Married to Rosalind Wellington for fifteen years. No children.

I shut the lights off and lay on the bed for a time in the near darkness, a little light coming in from the kitchen, even less coming in from the streetlights on Marlborough Street. I sipped a small sip of Black Bush. Irish whiskey was good for sipping carefully, alone, in silence. It was good for grief also, though I hadn't needed it lately. I took my glass and walked to my front window and looked down at Marlborough Street. Every moment of intense happiness in my life had been spent with Susan. Whenever I saw her I felt a thrill of excitement. If she went out to get the paper off the front porch, I was thrilled when she came back in. And yet as I stood looking down at the motionless street below me, I loved the solitude. Susan and I shared many nights, but we didn't live together. I've never known quite why. We tried it once, and it made us both unhappy. Maybe the thrill of seeing her was more intense because we didn't share a roof. We were very different. What we had in common was that we loved each other. What was different was everything else. She could feel deeply and think deeply, but she tended to rely more on the thinking. I was probably inclined somewhat the other way.

"If one is a bit insecure, despite all appearances," she had once said to me, "one tends to think ahead very carefully."

"And if one is not?" I had said.

"Then," she had said, "one tends to trust one's feelings and plow ahead, assuming one can handle whatever results."

"A nice balance would be good," I had said.

"It would," she had said. "And it would be rare."

I smiled. Where did the covert insecurity come from? Her first marriage had been very bad. But that marriage was probably a function of insecurity, not a cause. The cause probably lingered back in Swampscott, in the Hirsch family dynamics. Whatever it was, it was then, and we were now, and the hell with it.

On Marlborough Street, a man turned the corner from Arlington Street, walking a brisk Scottie on a leash. Late for walking the dog. Maybe he had trouble lasting through the night.

My glass was empty. I went to the kitchen and got more ice and poured in more whiskey and sat in my armchair by the cold fireplace in the living room and took a small swallow. It eased into my capillaries and moved pleasantly along my nerve patterns. *I have taken more from whiskey than whiskey has ever taken from me.*

There was a pattern here, someplace, in Prince's death. It wasn't clearly visible yet, but there was some kind of design in place that I couldn't fully get. It had to do with the Holocaust, and Jewish, and Dutch, and art. But if I knew some of the ingredients, I still didn't know the design, except that it might well be of darkness to appall. I was used to that. I'd spent most of my life looking around in dark places that were often appalling. But oddly, I was never really appalled. I looked where I needed to look to do what I did. And what was there was there. I'd done it too long to speculate much on why it was there. When I needed to, I could flatten out my emotional response until it was simply blank. I liked what I did, probably because I was good at it. And sometimes I won. Sometimes I slew the dragon and galloped away with the maiden. Sometimes I didn't. Sometimes the dragon survived. Sometimes I lost the maiden. But so far the dragon hadn't slain me . . . and I was never terminally appalled. And I was with Susan.

I smiled to myself and made a little self-congratulatory gesture with my whiskey glass.

"Sometimes solitary," I said to no one. "But never alone."

I celebrated that singular fact in the happy darkness until my glass was empty.

Then I went to bed.

30

In the morning, I stopped by the Boston Public Library on my way to work and picked up a copy of *Aesthetics and Greed in the Second Great War* and took it with me while I picked up two large coffees and a whole-wheat bagel and went up to my office.

I drank my coffee and ate my bagel, which was pretty good, and dipped into Prince's book. Which was not pretty good. He was an academic. He never used a short word when a long one would do nearly as well. His prose style was so pretentious that it obscured his meaning. After the first page I could feel my head beginning to nod. I plugged through the first chapter, taking solace in my coffee and my bagel, and stopped. I didn't want to solve his murder badly enough that I would read more than one chapter at a time. In chapter one, I learned that Germany had invaded the Netherlands in 1940.

I couldn't wait for chapter two to find out who won.

I checked out the length of the book and the approximate size of each chapter, and made a deal with myself that I'd read a chapter a day. More than that and I wouldn't know what I had read, anyway.

It was ten in the morning. I had read a chapter, eaten a bagel, and drunk two cups of Guatemalan coffee, and the day stretched out ahead of me like an empty road. I invoked Spenser's crime-stopper tip #5: When you have nothing else to do, follow someone.

I drove out to Walford and set up outside Missy Minor's dorm. It was not yet eleven. Many college students avoided classes that early in the day. Some, as I recall, avoided them altogether. But in most cases, they were just beginning to surface in the hour before lunch.

At about one-thirty in the afternoon, Missy Minor came out, ready to face the day. She was wearing her fleece-lined coat again. Very tight black jeans again, though not perhaps the same ones. The jeans were tucked into Uggs today. On her head was a white knit cap with a big white ball on top. The cap was pulled down carefully over her ears, allowing her blonde hair to frame her face. Warm yet fashionable. She was carrying no books as she cut across campus, with me discreetly behind her. She went into the library and up to the big reading room on the second floor. Missy went straight across the big room and sat down at an otherwise empty table across from a guy in a navy peacoat.

With my hands in my pockets and my head down, I went to the back end of the reading room, where there was a newspaper rack, got a *New York Times,* opened it up, and sat in a chair behind it, and peeked around.

The guy in the peacoat didn't look like a student. No shame to it. I didn't, either. And maybe he was an older student. He looked to be in his middle forties, with a flat, expressionless face and short blond hair. There was something about him that reminded me of the kind of guy I sometimes did business with. But it was an intangible something, and for all I knew, he could be a scholar of the eighteenth-century English novel.

As I watched, they leaned across the table toward each other and talked with their faces very close. It looked romantic, but they didn't touch. They talked intensely. She with animation. He was nearly motionless, except that he tapped his forefinger on the tabletop. They spoke for maybe fifteen minutes. Then she leaned back a little, as if she was going to stand. He put his right hand on her forearm and held her there.

They spoke for several more minutes. He was doing most of the talking. She was nodding. And she appeared to be pressing a little against the restraint of his hand. When he let her go, she stood and walked away. From where I sat, I couldn't read her expression. The man watched her walk across the reading room and out into the corridor and down the stairs. When she was out of sight, he sat quietly for a time, looking at nothing, slowly rubbing his chin with the back of his hand.

I stayed where I was behind my newspaper and waited. After a while he stopped rubbing his chin, and stood and walked out of the reading room. I gave him a minute and then put my newspaper back in its rack and strolled out after him. He was at the bottom of the stairs when I reached the top. I let him cross the big lobby to the front door before I started down. He had no reason to think he was being followed, so he had no reason to do anything tricky. And, of course, he was being tailed by an ace. I went down after him.

On the broad front steps of the library, I paused and took in some fresh air. Libraries always made me feel as if I'd been indoors too long. I saw my man across the street, heading toward a parking lot. I strolled after him. He got into a Toyota 4Runner and backed out. I recorded his license number in my steel-trap memory, and as soon as he was out of sight took out a little notepad and wrote it down. Just in time, before I forgot it.

31

The 4Runner was registered to Morton Lloyd with a Chestnut Hill address. Morton Lloyd was also the name of the lawyer that Prince had threatened Walford University with. And he was also the lawyer who represented the Hammond Museum, and it was through his recommendation that Prince got the job of negotiating the return of the painting. Seemed unlikely that there would be two Morton Lloyds in the same case.

I was meeting Rita Fiore for lunch at Locke-Ober, and was already seated when she came into the dining room wearing heels that told me she hadn't walked over from her office. The skirt of her gray suit was about mid-thigh, and everything fit her well. Her dark red hair was long and thick. Almost all the men in the place looked at her as she came in.

Those who didn't probably had a hormonal problem. I stood when she reached the table, and she gave me a kiss.

"Everyone in the place watched you come in," I said.

She smiled.

"I'm used to it," she said. "And I want a martini."

"Anything," I said.

"If only that were true," she said.

She ordered a Grey Goose martini on the rocks with a twist.

"What are you drinking?" she asked.

"Iced tea," I said.

"For a superhero," Rita said, "you are certainly a candy-ass drinker."

"I'm so ashamed," I said. "What's Morton Lloyd look like?"

"Haven't you seen him?" Rita said.

"Once," I said. "Tall, kind of heavy. Black hair combed back, lotta gel, kind of a wedge-shaped face, big mustache with some gray in it. Maybe fifty-five."

"That would be Mort," Rita said.

"Okay," I said. "Same guy I met at the Hammond Museum. Not the same guy driving the car."

The martini arrived. Rita drank some.

"Nothing like vodka and vermouth to knit up the raveled sleeve of care," she said. "What car?"

"A car registered to Lloyd," I said.

"But he wasn't driving it?"

"No," I said.

"I talked with him," Rita said. "Says he barely knows Prince. Says Prince came to him through a regular client; said he feared being slandered by Walford University, and if he were, he'd want to sue them, and he wanted to know that Mort would represent him."

"Lloyd recommended him to the museum to negotiate the return of the painting," I said.

"Really?" Rita said. "Perhaps Mort was not being entirely open and honest with me."

"I'm shocked," I said.

The waiter came for our orders, we gave them, and Rita asked for another martini.

"Mort says he brushed Prince off," Rita said. "Says if they slander him, he should give Mort a call."

"Whatever the truth, it scared Walford off," I said.

"And if somebody checked on him," Rita said, "he had consulted Lloyd, and Lloyd had, sort of, agreed to represent him."

"Yep," I said. "Who was the client who sent Prince to Lloyd?"

"He said it was something called the Herzberg Foundation. Mort was evasive as to what it was. All I could get was that it was something to do with the Holocaust. And it might have been earlier than I thought. He was vague on that, too. I frankly don't think he wanted to tell me anything," Rita said, and smiled. "But you know how I can be."

"I do," I said. "He is their legal counsel?"

"Yes," Rita said. "He seems happy with that. I gather he's on retainer."

"Is he a stand-up guy?" I said.

"Mort? Stand-up. Yes," Rita said. "I'd say he is. But that would be true only if he were standing up for Mort."

I nodded.

"The two guys who ambushed me both had an Auschwitz ID number tattooed on their arm," I said.

"My God, Auschwitz was sixty years ago," Rita said.

"More," I said.

"I don't do math," Rita said. "I'm a girl."

"And the world is a better place for it," I said.

"Of course it is," Rita said. "How old were these guys?"

"Late thirties," I said. "They both had the same number."

"So it's, like, symbolic," Rita said.

"Or something," I said. "Now I see a guy visiting Prince's old girlfriend, and he's driving a car registered to a lawyer who represents some kind of Holocaust foundation."

"Convoluted," Rita said.

"It is," I said.

"But you can't ignore it," Rita said.

"No, I can't."

"Is it a real serial number," Rita said. "The tattoo?"

"It looks right," I said. "You know, the right amount of numbers and such."

"Maybe it can be traced."

"Quirk's working on that," I said.

"You ID'd the two guys who tried to kill you?"

"Not yet."

"You got any physical evidence linking the attempt on you to the Prince killing?"

"No."

"But you know it is," Rita said.

"Yes," I said. "You were a prosecutor. You know when you know."

"I remember," Rita said.

"Prince was Jewish," I said. "His real name, according to his wife, was Ascher Prinz. His father was in a concentration camp."

"Which one?"

"His wife doesn't know," I said. "They all sound the same."

"The concentration camps all sound the same?"

"What she told me," I said. "She's a poet."

"The hell she is," Rita said.

"She's writing an epic poem, she says, about how her husband's death has impacted her."

"Can't wait," Rita said.

I was having a lobster club sandwich. Rita had a big plate of wienerschnitzel and a glass of wine. How she could drink two martinis and a glass of Riesling and eat a large plate of fried veal for lunch was a puzzle to me.

"How can you eat and drink like that," I said, "and continue to look like you do."

She smiled.

"Sex burns a lot of calories," she said.

"Wow," I said.

She smiled.

"I'll help you with this any way I can. I'm a good lawyer, for a girl."

"'For a girl,'" I said. "When you were prosecuting in Norfolk, them defense lawyers used to call you Rita Shark."

"They were referring to my sleek and sinuous grace," she said. "But I mean it. I don't like people trying to kill you. If I can help, I will. We have some pretty good resources at Cone, Oakes."

"And you're one of them," I said.

She cut off a smallish bite of wienerschnitzel and chewed and swallowed and smiled at me again.

"I know," she said.

32

After lunch, Rita went back to work, and I went to see Quirk. Belson was with him in his office.

"Got an ID on your two assailants," Quirk said.

"And they are?" I said.

"Two Dutch nationals," Quirk said. "Mercenaries. What's the names, Frank?"

"One's Joost. The other one's Van Meer," Belson said. "You care which is which?"

"Not right now," I said.

"Joost is thirty-four, Van Meer is thirty-five. They weren't in our system, so we tried Interpol and there they were."

"You dig that up?" I said to Belson.

"Yep."

"Frank Belson," I said, "international detective."

"Long-distance phone caller," Belson said.

"And you're still a sergeant?"

"They don't promote you for doing a good job," Belson said. "They promote you for scoring on the lieutenant's test."

"So take the test," I said.

"He won't," Quirk said.

"No?" I said.

"I am what I am, and if that's good, I should be promoted. I'm not taking no fucking test," Belson said.

Quirk grinned.

"Frank's a great cop," Quirk said. "But nobody's arguing he ain't a hard-on."

"I don't believe I've ever heard anyone argue that," I said.

"You want to hear about these two guys you killed?" Belson said. "Or you and the captain want to keep having fun?"

"Joost and Van Meer," I said. "Tell me."

"Served in the Royal Dutch Army. Airborne brigade. Fought in Iraq and Afghanistan."

"There were Dutch troops in Iraq and Afghanistan?"

"What am I," Belson said, *Meet the Fucking Press*? That's what Interpol told me."

"Learn something every day," I said.

"Probably not in your case," Belson said. "They got out, served with the Israeli army, some kind of commando unit. Maybe covert ops. Got out of that and started a private security agency, Joost and Van Meer. Then they went off Interpol's radar."

"Why is Interpol interested?" I said.

"They're wanted for questioning in the murder of some French guy, owned an art gallery," Belson said with no expression.

"Art," I said.

"Yep," Belson said.

"What do the French cops tell you?" I said.

"Guy had their name on an appointment calendar for the day he was killed."

"Not much," I said.

"Enough to want to interview them," Belson said.

"True," I said. "Anybody got any thoughts about the tattoos?"

"Nobody knows anything about that," Belson said.

"Puts us in good company," I said.

"We're talking with folks at the Holocaust Museum in D.C.," Quirk said.

"Progress?"

"They're trying to run down an outfit in Germany. Supposed to have everything about the Third Reich."

"Is that hard to do?" I said.

"Apparently," Quirk said. "And it's not just a matter of locating the stuff. It's getting access to it with somebody fluent in German."

"American embassy?"

"I'm sure mine would be the first call they'd take," Quirk said.

"We got art, and Dutch stuff, and Jewish stuff, and

German stuff, and Holocaust stuff, and a guy got killed on Route Two, and a guy got killed in France," I said. "We figure this out, I'll get promoted to lieutenant."

"Maybe not," Quirk said.

"Not if you don't take the freakin' test," Belson said.

Quirk smiled.

"Excellent point, Frank," he said.

33

Susan and Pearl came for breakfast on Saturday morning.
"Hurry up," Susan said. "Eat something quick. Otto
and his mom are in town, and they're going to meet us for a
playdate."

"What time?" I said.

"Eleven," Susan said. "She e-mailed me. Isn't that great?
Said we should meet by the little bridge in the Public
Garden."

"I don't think we have to hurry much," I said. "It's eight-
thirty. You want coffee."

"Yes, but let's not dawdle over it."

Pearl had gone directly to the couch and assumed her normal position. Which was prone. She looked to me as though
she would be content to dawdle the whole day. Despite her

excitement, Susan was able to eat some homemade corn bread with blackberry jam and drink a cup of coffee. I had the same thing, only more, plus some orange juice. Susan checked her watch every couple of minutes. Otherwise, she was very civilized. Susan in a hurry can be something of a tempest.

"How," she said quietly, looking fully at me, the way she does, "is your case coming about the murder and the stolen picture."

"It gives me a headache," I said.

"Do they know who the men were that tried to kill you?"

"Couple of Dutch mercenaries," I said. "Joost and Van Meer."

"Do you know why they wanted to kill you?"

"No," I said. "I mean, they probably wanted to kill me because they'd been employed to. But who employed them and why?" I shook my head.

She sipped her coffee and looked at her watch.

"Is there any way I can help," she said.

"Actually, yeah, maybe," I said. "I need to talk with an expert in seventeenth-century low-country art, somebody got no stake in this case."

"I don't know anyone like that at this minute," Susan said. "But I have a Ph.D. from Harvard."

"So you'll find somebody."

"Of course."

She checked her watch. According to the clock on my stove, it was five minutes to ten. Actually, the clock, being digital, like they almost all are, read nine-fifty-six. But I was pretty loyal to the old ways, and I translated and rounded off, just as I had in the happy years before digital. On the couch, Pearl was snoring calmly.

Susan put her coffee cup on my counter.

"I think I'll get her started," Susan said.

"Good idea," I said. "How long you think it'll take you to get there?"

"Oh, I don't know, five minutes maybe?"

"Which will make it approximately ten o'clock," I said.

"Yes, but I don't want to be late."

"You're always late," I said.

"Not on Pearl's second date," Susan said. "What kind of a mother would I be?"

She was playing, and we both knew she was. And we both knew also that she wasn't altogether and entirely playing. We cleaned up the breakfast, put the dishes in the washer, and headed over to the Public Garden. It was ten-fifteen.

34

At eleven-oh-three Susan and I were leaning on the railing of the bridge over the frozen pond where late the sweet swan boats plied. Pearl was snuffling through the vestigial snow at the Arlington Street end of the bridge, alert for a discarded doughnut. No one would, of course, discard a doughnut, so I knew her search was aimless. Still, I liked to let her cultivate her hunting impulse. I didn't want to impose our realistic limits on the soar of her imagination.

"'To strive,'" I said to Susan, "'to seek . . . and not to yield.'"

"Of course," Susan said.

Pearl stopped suddenly and lifted her head. She did an olfactory scan of the air, head lifted, short tail out straight, body motionless and rigid, one forepaw raised. Then she put the forepaw down carefully, posed like that for another few seconds, and exploded on a dead run toward Boylston Street. Coming like a tidal wave through the gate from Boylston Street was Otto. They met in exuberant collision somewhere near the far end of the frozen swan boat pond. Otto bowled Pearl over and then tripped over her and fell down, too, and they rolled on the ground, mock fighting, with their tails wagging ferociously. Otto's mother was there, with a good-sized man, who turned out to be Otto's father. Otto's father had a definite New York City look about him.

Both dogs got their feet under them and faced each other with their back ends elevated, front paws extended, chests near the ground, growling lasciviously, and head faking at each other. Then suddenly they straightened and began to dash in widening gyres about the Public Garden as pedestrians dodged and some cringed. Susan and I and Otto's mom and dad stood watching like chaperones at a freshman dance.

"They're adorable," Otto's mother said.

"Absolutely," Pearl's mother said.

There was a Scottie and a Jack Russell off leash in the garden as well as Otto and Pearl, and they made a kind of halfhearted attempt to get in on the frolic, but they couldn't keep up, and neither Pearl nor Otto paid them any mind.

"We take him almost everywhere," Otto's mom said. "Do you like pictures?"

"I love pictures," Susan said.

Otto's mom took out a digital camera and began to

click through the stored pictures as Susan leaned over, look-ing at them and saying "Oh my God" and "Totally adorable," and things like that. What made me smile was that I knew she meant it. She loved looking at other people's pictures, especially pictures of Pearl's first real romance.

"Stop there," Susan said. "Where is this?"

"Oh, that's a gala we took him to," Otto's mom said. "We posed him in front of that painting because we thought it looked a little like him."

Susan said to me, "Look at this."

I looked. It was a picture of Otto, beaming and self-confident, in front of the painting of a prosperous-looking seventeenth-century merchant who did, in fact, look a little like Otto.

"Frans Hals?" I said.

"Yes," Otto's mom said. "It was a benefit for a small museum in New York of seventeenth-century Dutch art."

"Same period when they founded New Amsterdam," I said.

"Exactly," Otto's mom said.

As they had on their last meeting, Pearl and Otto finally burned themselves out and came and flopped down with their tongues hanging from their mouths. Otto's dad bent over and patted them both.

"Do you know people at this museum?" Susan said.

"Oh, yes," Otto's mom said. "I'm on the board."

"Is there anyone at this museum with a specialized knowledge of Dutch art, and the art business?"

"Sure." She looked at Otto's dad. "That lovely man, with the salt-and-pepper beard. You know, Carl something?"

"Carl Trachtman," Otto's dad said. "Probably the leading expert in the world in low-country art."

Susan nodded at me.

"Do you suppose he'd talk with the big ugly one here?"

"He talks to me," Otto's dad said.

I grinned at him.

"Then I'm golden," I said.

Otto's dad smiled and took out a cell phone.

"We're practically in-laws," he said. "I'll give him a call."

"See," Susan said. "I told you I'd find somebody."

The two dogs were lying between us, Pearl's head resting on Otto's.

"She has a Ph.D. from Harvard," I said to Otto's dad.

"Wow!" he said, and punched up a number on his cell phone.

35

The Museum of the Dutch Renaissance was on upper Madison Avenue in Manhattan, several blocks north of the Viand Coffee Shop. The museum was a lovely low building that had once been a church, and Carl Trachtman was the curator.

"Otto is a glorious dog," Trachtman said when I sat down.

"So is Pearl," I said.

Trachtman smiled.

"Proud parents," he said.

"You have a dog?" I said.

"I do," Trachtman said. "A Piebald dachshund named Vermeer. We call her Vee."

"She glorious?" I said.

Trachtman smiled.

"Completely," he said.

"Many dogs are," I said.

Trachtman went around behind his ornate antique desk, doubtless of low-country origin, and sat down and smiled.

"Now that we've exchanged bona fides," Trachtman said, "let me say that I'm very familiar with this case. I've followed it with great interest. My great hope is that it wasn't *Lady with a Finch* that exploded."

"Wasn't enough left to test," I said. "But for what it's worth, I don't think it was destroyed."

"Its life has been so hazardous," Trachtman said, "for the nearly four hundred years since Hermenszoon painted it."

He looked at my card.

"You're a *private* detective," he said.

"Yes, sir," I said.

"What is your interest in the case?"

"I was Dr. Prince's bodyguard when he got killed," I said.

Trachtman nodded slowly. He was a smallish overweight man with a Vandyke beard and receding gray hair.

"And you wish to get what? Revenge?"

"You might call it that," I said. "I cannot let people murder somebody I was hired to protect."

Trachtman nodded.

"So it would be, perhaps, more about you than poor Dr. Prince," he said.

"Probably," I said. "But whatever it is, I'm on it, and I'm not going to let go of it."

"Determination is not a bad thing," Trachtman said. "Properly applied. How would you like me to help you."

"Tell me about the painting, tell me about Prince; you may correctly assume that I know nothing."

"I suspect you know more than you pretend to," Trachtman said.

"Hard to know less," I said.

"Where shall I begin," Trachtman said. "Background on seventeenth-century low-country realism? What makes this painting so special? What makes Hermenszoon so special?"

"Probably a paragraph of that stuff, so I can sound smart talking about the case," I said. "But mostly I'm interested in the history of the painting and whatever you may know about Ashton Prince."

Trachtman leaned back a little in his chair, as if he was about to enjoy a good meal.

"Frans Hermenszoon," he said, "had he lived, would have been as widely known today as Rembrandt or Vermeer, with whom he was contemporary. He was in many ways an exemplar of the best of everything in seventeenth-century Dutch painting. Use of light, and meticulous realism, and an understated commentary on human, by which he would have meant Dutch, existence. *Lady with a Finch*, for instance, in its stillness and beauty and meticulous realism, seems permanent. Yet, of course, we know that the bird will fly off any moment. So with human life, Hermenszoon seems to suggest."

"He died young?" I asked, just to avoid passivity.

"Not yet thirty," Trachtman said. "Stabbed through the eye, apparently in a drunken brawl."

"Like Christopher Marlowe," I said.

"My, my," Trachtman said. "You do know more than you let on."

"I live alone," I said. "I read a lot."

"No wife?" Trachtman said.

"No," I said. "Though I have kept intimate company with the girl of my dreams for most of my adult life."

"But not married?"

"No."

"Why?" Trachtman said.

"I don't know."

"It is good to have someone," Trachtman said. "I'm glad you do."

"How many paintings are there by Hermenszoon?" I said.

"In his lifetime there were perhaps eight. To the best of our knowledge, only *Lady with a Finch* survives."

"How do you know there used to be eight?"

"Transaction records, diaries, letters," Trachtman said. "Usual sources."

"So being the one and only makes it even more valuable than it otherwise might be?"

"The painting is a great work of art," Trachtman said. "It's priceless."

"And its pricelessness is enhanced by its singularity," I said.

Trachtman smiled.

"Well put," he said.

"Is there a history?"

"Certainly," Trachtman said. "It remained in the Her-menszoon family something like two hundred years, then was acquired by a wealthy Jewish family in Amsterdam named Herzberg. It remained in the Herzberg family until 1940, when Judah Herzberg and his entire family were arrested by the Nazis and sent to Auschwitz. The Nazis also confiscated the vast and priceless art collection that the family had maintained. After the war, some of the paintings were recovered and identified with the Herzberg family by a special unit of the U.S. military established to deal with stolen art. But the entire family had perished in Auschwitz, except a son, Isaac, who would have been about nine when he arrived in Auschwitz. No one could find the boy, who in 1945 would have been fourteen. He had disappeared into the tidal wave of refugees, many of them homeless, which inundated Europe at the time."

"What happened to the paintings," I said, "when they couldn't find anyone to return them to?"

"They were kept in a sort of holding facility and distributed to museums or sold to private collectors. The army took surprisingly good care of them, being, you know, military men. But inevitably some just re-disappeared."

"Ever hear of the Herzberg Foundation?" I said.

"No," Trachtman said. "I haven't. What is it?"

"Just a name," I said. "Came up in discussion. Probably a coincidence."

"If it had to do with seventeenth-century Dutch painting," Trachtman said, "I would know of it."

"Of course," I said. "Did the Hammond Museum get the painting from the army?"

"In 1949," Trachtman said.

"They never found the Herzberg kid?"

"There have been several claimants," Trachtman said. "But none has been able to prove his lineage."

"Hard to do if your entire family is wiped out and you're in a death camp for five years."

"Very hard," Trachtman said.

We were silent for a moment.

"When was he last heard of?" I said.

"He is on a list of surviving prisoners released from Auschwitz by the Russians," Trachtman said. "That would date to 1945. We have no further record."

"So he could have died six months later," I said.

"Could," Trachtman said.

"Or he could be alive and living in Zanzibar," I said.

"Could," Trachtman said.

I nodded.

"Tell me what you can about Ashton Prince," I said.

36

A woman came into Trachtman's office with some coffee and cookies on a small tray.

Trachtman introduced her.

"My assistant, Ibby Moser," he said. "Say hello to Mr. Spenser, Ibby."

She said hello and put the tray down.

"Ibby's cookies are amazing," Trachtman said. "Try one." I took one and ate half of it. It was peanut butter.

"Amazing," I said.

We all smiled, and Ibby left.

"A mid-afternoon ritual," Trachtman said. "Every day. I never know what kind of cookies it will be."

"Nice ritual," I said. "Ashton Prince?"

"Ashton is odd," Trachtman said. "On the one hand, he is a first-rate scholar of low-country realism. An expert."

"As expert as you?" I said.

"His expertise may not be as broad," Trachtman said. "I am a bit of a generalist. But in his areas of specialization, it is deeper. He is . . . or was, I suppose I should say . . . the greatest authority I know of, far greater than I, on Franz Hermenszoon."

"Doesn't matter what tense you use," I said. "We both know he's dead."

Trachtman smiled.

"I like to be precise," he said. "There was also an odd sort of collateral specialty. . . . He was unsurpassed in the identification of forgeries in the art of the period."

"Which is to say Dutch art in the time of Rembrandt," I said.

"More or less," Trachtman said.

"You said that on the one hand he was what you've just described," I said. "How about the other hand?"

Trachtman smiled and shook his head.

"This will be, I suppose, a bit subjective," he said.

"Many things are," I said.

He nodded.

"There was something deeply fraudulent about Ashton," he said. "I didn't know him well, but we had met at conferences and such, and I knew his work. But there was something . . . artificial about him. As if he were, oh, I don't know, performing. Like someone in a drama whose acting shows through."

"I think actors call that 'indicating.'"

"Really," Trachtman said. "Are you a theater buff?"

"No, but I have a friend who is a performer."

"You appear to be one on whom nothing is lost," Trachtman said.

"Though often wasted," I said. "Do you know anything about his personal life?"

"Nothing," he said. "Nothing. That's part of it. Look at you. I've never met you before. We've talked for perhaps half an hour. And I know that you are unmarried and live alone, but you are in a committed relationship with a woman of whom you are quite fond, and you have a dog."

"We share a dog," I said.

"I knew nothing of Ashton," Trachtman said. "He dressed like some sort of caricature of an art professor. He had a fluty accent, as if he had gone to an upper-class English boarding school."

"I know," I said. "I spent time with him. Do you know if Ashton Prince is his real name?"

"As far as I know," Trachtman said. "But if it weren't, I wouldn't be startled. He seems just like the kind of man that would change his name . . . and Ashton Prince is the kind of name he'd change it to."

"Anything else about him bothers you?" I said.

"Walford," Trachtman said. "He stayed, for God's sake, at Walford."

"Not a good thing?" I said.

"Walford is all right," he said. "But it is not a first-rate art department, neither in composition nor history. It does not value artistic scholarship in the way that, say, Yale would. Or Brown. Prince was not as free as he might have been some-place else to do scholarship. He had no research support. He always had classes to teach."

"Salary?" I said.

"He would have been paid more had he taught at a major university."

"And he was good enough to upgrade?" I said.

"Absolutely," Trachtman said.

"Any idea why he stayed?"

"In many people I would speculate inertia," Trachtman said. "But Ashton Prince was one of the great forensic art scholars in the world in his period. People who achieve that kind of expertise are rarely inert."

"Hard to generalize," I said.

"Yes."

"But he had the credentials to work at better schools for more money and fewer teaching hours and more research support."

"He did indeed."

"And he apparently chose not to," I said.

"Yes," Trachtman said. "That is a puzzle."

"Maybe he liked teaching," I said. "Maybe he wanted to be in the classroom."

"I am, myself," Trachtman said, "a reformed academic. In

my years at the trade I never met anyone who didn't want his or her teaching load to be smaller."

"So they can do more research?" I said.

"No," Trachtman said. "Because they don't like to teach. It's hard work if you really do it."

"Most things are," I said. "What would they prefer to do?"

"Sit about in the faculty lounge, drinking bad coffee and discussing intensely matters of great import with which they have no active engagement."

"Frees their mind," I said, "to romp with the mind of God."

"Who said that?" Trachtman said.

"Nick Carraway, in *The Great Gatsby*," I said. "Did Prince seem like that to you?"

"No," Trachtman said. "He seemed a man who might actually want to be engaged."

"Be my guess, too," I said.

We spent the rest of the afternoon at it, but nothing much else surfaced. So I went back to the Carlyle, which was always one of my New York indulgences, along with the Four Seasons restaurant and the Bronx Zoo. I had a couple of drinks from the minibar, ordered room service, called Susan, and had a pretty good time.

In the morning I had breakfast in the dining room and got my car from the garage and drove home straight to Susan's house. Where I spent the night.

37

Susan had early appointments, and I left her to them and went home at about seven-thirty. In the Back Bay all the streets have a public alley behind them, and the alleys are numbered. The one behind my building was number 21. I pulled into it off Arlington Street and parked in my spot behind my building. There was a back entrance, but I always liked to walk around and go in the front door. It was a good-looking street, and I liked that I lived there. I'd gotten the place when it was far cheaper than it would be now, and I'd worked on it during slow moments in the sleuthing business, so it was pretty much just the way I liked it. Actually, it was probably more the way Susan liked it, and I didn't mind.

One of the collateral benefits of having someone try to kill you is that it makes you alert . . . unless they succeed.

And as I walked to my door, I noticed a maroon Lexus sedan parked across the street from my building. The passenger-side window went down as I walked up Marlborough Street, and a cigarette flipped into the street. It was cold, but the motor wasn't running. So somebody in there was sitting in a cold car. It could be that he didn't want to attract my attention to the white exhaust that would tail up from the car if the motor was running. Might be that he was waiting for someone and didn't want to waste gas, or pollute the atmosphere by letting his car idle.

If he was waiting for me, he probably expected me to come out of my building in front of him, and not walk up the street behind him. Or he might be killing time until a meeting that he didn't want to be early for. The car had tinted windows, and I couldn't see in. So I paid it no apparent attention and turned into my front walk and up the low stairs. The entry to my building had a glass door, and I could see the Lexus reflected in it. There was no movement. I opened the door and went in and looked back out covertly. Nothing.

I shrugged and went to my apartment. The door seemed as always. Still, no sense being careless. I put my overnight bag on the floor and took out my gun while I unlocked the door. I felt a little paranoid, but that was quite a bit better than feeling a little dead.

My apartment was undisturbed. No one was in it. I retrieved my overnight bag and locked my front door and headed to the front windows to see if anything was shaking down below. As I passed the open door to my bedroom I tossed my suitcase on the bed and was a step past the doorway when it landed and the bed exploded.

Scraps of mattress and bed frame surged through my door and scattered on my living-room floor. I stepped back a little and peeked around the doorjamb. The bed was gone. Beyond that, there was surprisingly little damage. The bomb had been intended to kill only me. It must have been under the mattress, which had muffled its force and sound. I went to my living-room window and looked down.

The Lexus had pulled out of its parking spot and was approaching Berkeley Street. I got the license-plate number. Then I called the cops and walked back into my bedroom and looked at the wreckage.

38

Belson and I sat at my kitchen counter and watched the technicians do whatever it was they did.

"These guys are pretty good," Belson said.

"I know."

"They keep at it, they might get you."

"I think the best bet is to catch them before they do," I said.

Belson nodded.

"Good idea," he said. "The license-plate number you got from the Lexus is assigned to a Volkswagen Passat. Owner is Laurie Hanlon. We'll check her out, but sounds a lot like a stolen plate to me."

"If it had anything to do with the bomb blast in the first place," I said.

"If it's a stolen plate," Belson said, "it would make me think that they did."

"Yeah, sat out there for however long," I said, "waiting to make sure the bomb went off."

"One of your neighbors takes her kid out in his carriage couple times a day, says the car's been there for several days. Sometimes, she says, another car would pull up and a guy would get out and swap places with the guy in the Lexus."

"Working in shifts," I said.

"Rivera, the bomb-squad guy, says the kind of charge they rigged, to just destroy the bed and its occupant, is pretty sophisticated."

"Can they tell anything else about it?"

"Nothing much to look at," Belson said. "Maybe when they get the scraps into the lab."

"We knew they had a bomber on staff," I said. "The thing that blew Prince up wasn't a bunch of nails in a pipe."

"True," Belson said. "You know how they got in here?"

"No."

"You've looked?" Belson said.

"What do I do for a living," I said. "Sell watches out of the trunk of my car?"

"You've looked."

"I see no sign of forced entry," I said.

"We haven't, either," Belson said. "Anybody got a key to the place besides Susan?"

"Hawk," I said.

"Where is he?"

"Central Asia," I said.

"Central Asia? Doing what?"

"What he does," I said. "It's got something to do with Ives, the government guy. You know Ives?"

"The spook," Belson said.

"Yes."

Belson shook his head slowly.

"Anybody else?"

"Nope. Just Hawk and Susan."

"She's okay?"

"Left her at seven-thirty this morning," I said. "She was fine."

"Why don't I ask Cambridge to send a car up there, just to check," Belson said.

"Yes," I said.

He stood and went to the other end of the living room, where he took out a cell phone and talked for maybe five minutes. Then he came back.

"Cambridge will send a car up. I explained a little of the deal. They'll actually talk to her, make sure she's okay."

I nodded.

One of the uniformed cops, a young one, came into my apartment.

"Sergeant," he said.

"You got something, Stevie?" Belson said.

The young cop looked at me.

"He's on our side," Belson said. "For the moment, at least."

Stevie nodded.

"Got a stiff in the cellar," he said. "Hispanic male, maybe forty, forty-five, shot once in the back of the head. Got a tattoo on his right biceps says Rosa."

"Francisco," I said. "The super."

Belson nodded.

"He have a passkey?"

"Sure," I said.

"That's probably how they got in," he said.

I nodded.

"Take some scientists down there, Stevie," Belson said. "I'll be right there."

He looked at me

"You wanna take a look?"

"I would," I said.

And we headed to the cellar.

39

Francisco had been a good guy, and clever with his hands. He could fix a lot of stuff. Now he was facedown on the floor of his basement workroom with a small, dark hole at the base of his skull, in a pool of his blood dried and blackened on the floor.

"Keys?" Belson said.

Stevie shook his head. "Haven't seen any."

"Normally carried them in front, hooked to a belt loop," I said. "Large bunch. You could hear him coming. They may be under him."

"Turn him," Belson said.

And a couple of technicians turned him up on his side.

The bullet had apparently exited his forehead and made a much larger hole, from which the blood had come. The keys were on his belt loop. The technicians let him back down as he had been. Belson squatted on his haunches and looked at the bullet hole.

"Big caliber," he said.

"Big enough," I said.

Belson stood up.

"Bell marked *Super* out front?" Belson said.

"Yes," I said.

"So they ring the bell," Belson said to whatever he was looking at in the middle distance. "He lets them in. They point a gun at him, and since they don't know the layout here, he takes them to your place and opens the door."

"Then they walk him to the cellar and into his office," I said, "and execute him."

"No witness," Belson said.

He appeared to be staring blankly at nothing. But I'd known him a long time, and I knew he was seeing everything in the room and could give you an inventory of it a week later. A Homicide dick named Perpetua came into the room.

"Look around, Pep," Belson said. "When you're done, come talk to me."

Perpetua nodded and took out a notebook.

To me, Belson said, "Let's you and me go someplace and talk."

"*Mi casa, su casa*," I said.

We went up from the basement and sat on the stairs between the first and second floor.

"Couple things," Belson said.

His cell phone rang. Belson listened, nodding slightly. At one point he smiled.

"She did, huh?" he said.

More listening.

"Thanks," Belson said, and broke the connection.

"Susan's fine," he said. "She was with a patient and wasn't pleased about the interruption."

"She speak sharply to anyone."

"I believe she called the prowl-car guy a 'fucking asshole,'" Belson said.

"That would be my Sweet Potato," I said.

"Cruiser will stay there, anyway, out front, for the day, at least."

"Probably make some of her patients nervous," I said.

"You want me to pull the cruiser off?" Belson said.

"No," I said.

"Okay," Belson said. "Coupla things. One, you must be getting very close to finding out something they don't want you to know."

"Seems so," I said.

"You know what it is?"

"I'm developing some theories," I said.

"Good. We'll talk about that," Belson said. "But right now, I figure that they aren't going to quit."

"They don't appear to be quitters," I said.

"No," Belson said. "But right at the moment they probably think they killed you."

"They probably do," I said.

"Might be smart to let them keep thinking so," Belson said.

"You have a plan?" I said.

"About half a plan," Belson said. "Say we slip you out the back way, and you stay in a motel or someplace?"

"No," I said.

"No?" Belson said.

"Frank," I said. "The only connection we got with them is their attempts to kill me. They think I'm dead and we lose that."

"For crissake," Belson said. "You hadn't tossed your overnight bag on the bed, you would be dead."

"But that wasn't just luck," I said. "I tossed it because I had spotted the guy in the car outside and was in a hurry to get a better look through my front window."

"That's weak," Belson said. "You think you can keep them from killing you until we catch them."

"Yes."

"You're fucking insane," Belson said.

"Yeah, but I have access to a good shrink," I said.

Belson nodded.

"Bedroom will have to be cleaned up," Belson said. "Window will have to be replaced. And the super isn't gonna do it."

"True," I said.

"And you'll need a new bed."

"Also true," I said.

"So you'll have to go someplace for a few days at least," Belson said. "I can slide you out the back way in case anyone is trying to tail you."

"If someone's trying to tail me," I said, "let's go out the front door and let him, and maybe we can catch him."

"Nobody's gonna tail us without one of us spotting the tail."

"Not possible," I said. "And if he makes a move at me, you can throw yourself into the line of fire."

"That is absolutely one of my favorite parts of police work," Belson said.

"Especially," I said, "if it's me you're taking the bullet for."

"Especially," Belson said. "But just in case nobody tails us and we don't catch him, and I don't take a bullet for you, how about backup?"

I shook my head.

"Vinnie?" Belson said.

"Nope."

"West Coast guy, Latino, helped you save my life when I got shot," Belson said.

"Chollo," I said.

"How about him?" Belson said. "Or the big queer from Georgia."

"Tedy Sapp," I said.

"Maybe one of them?"

I shook my head.

"This one's mine," I said.

Belson was silent for a while, nodding slowly.

Then he said, "Yeah."

40

I put my spare weaponry in a duffel bag and hauled it down
the stairs to Belson's car, which was double-parked in front
of my house.

"No suitcase?" Belson said.

"I keep stuff at Susan's," I said.

We got in. There was no sign of a tail.

"So you got a theory about what they don't want you
to find?"

"'Theory' is too strong," I said. "More like a guess."

"Guess is better than nothing," Belson said.

We turned right onto Berkeley Street and stopped for the
light at Beacon.

"There's an operation called the Herzberg Foundation,
to which Lloyd, the lawyer who recommended Prince to the

Hammond Museum, is a legal counsel. The Frans Hermens-zoon painting, *Lady with a Finch,* which was stolen from the Hammond Museum, whose attorney is Morton Lloyd, was owned at one point by a Dutch Jewish family named Herzberg."

The light changed. We crossed Beacon and went out onto Storrow Drive westbound.

"In 1940," I said, "after the Nazis conquered the Netherlands, the Herzbergs were arrested by the Gestapo and sent to Auschwitz, where all but the youngest son died. The great art collection of the Herzberg family was confiscated by the Nazis, including *Lady with a Finch.* The son was liberated in 1945 by the Russians, and disappeared."

"Dutch, Jewish, Holocaust, Herzberg," Belson said. "And artwork."

"So far," I said.

"You talk with Lloyd yet?"

"No, but Rita Fiore has."

"Good-looking redhead?" Belson said. "Used to be a prosecutor in Norfolk County?"

"Yep."

"She talk to him before or after they tried to hit you?"

"Yes," I said.

"Find out," Belson said.

"I will," I said.

The river was on our right; no one was on it or in it. No sculls training for the Head of the Charles Regatta. No college crews readying for the season. No ducks, no geese, no loons, no cormorants, no seagulls, no sailboats, no canoes, no kayaks, just the gray water, looking cold, with ice formed along the riverbanks, where the current wasn't as strong.

"You want me to talk to Lloyd?" Belson said. "The more we're in it, the more it defuses their reasons to kill you."

"And the more we lose that connection," I said.

"We'll lose it altogether, they scrag you," Belson said.

"I'll try to prevent that," I said.

"And you'll talk to Lloyd?" Belson said.

"Both," I said.

41

When Susan came up from the office, I was sitting on the couch with Pearl, drinking scotch and soda with a lot of ice. Susan kept some for me. She wouldn't drink it.

"How nice," she said when she saw me.

"What's for eats?" I said.

"You're in luck," she said. "I had friends over the other night. There's cheese and fruit, and adorable little dinner rolls, and, I think, some cold chicken left, too. And Iron Horse champagne."

"Zowie," I said. "How adorable, exactly, are the dinner rolls."

"You'll see," she said. "Mind if I unwind with a little wine before I set the table?"

"I was hoping you would," I said.

Susan got some pinot grigio and brought it to the couch and sat on the side of me where Pearl was not.

"There's a police car parked outside," Susan said.

"Cambridge?" I sat.

"There was a Cambridge one," Susan said. "Now it's a state police cruiser."

"Healy," I said.

"You'll explain," she said.

"I will."

We each sipped our drink.

Then she said, "So it is not just unbridled lust that brings you here."

"Well, that, too," I said.

"But there's something else," Susan said.

"Yes."

"Unbridled lust I'm used to," Susan said. "Tell me about the something else."

She listened quietly while I did. People had tried to kill me before. She wasn't exactly used to it, but she knew it was part of the package. But it wasn't anything she liked.

When I got through, she put her wineglass on the coffee table and put her arms around me and pressed her face into my neck. I put my arm around her. Finally she took in a deep breath and let it out and sat back.

She smiled at me.

"Just because you're a fugitive doesn't mean you can lie in bed with me and watch basketball all night," she said.

"I hate basketball. One of the many reasons we don't live together is that I don't like to watch what you like, and vice versa."

"It's more fundamental than that," I said. "I like the TV off; you like it on."

She nodded.

"You won't let them kill you," she said.

"I will not," I said.

"I believe you," she said. "You never have."

I got up and made another drink. And poured some more wine for Susan.

When I sat back down, I put my arm around her, and she rested her head against my shoulder. Pearl looked vaguely annoyed.

"Hey," I said to Pearl. "Did I give you a big look when you were flirting your brains out with Otto?"

Pearl remained unabashed. She lapped her muzzle a couple of times and continued the look as she settled back down and put her chin on my thigh.

"You know what struck me when you were telling your story?" Susan said.

I shook my head.

"They are obviously dangerous people. They tried to kill you twice now, and they killed the poor super, just because he was inconvenient."

"He was a witness," I said.

"I mean, they could have blown up the whole building."

"Could," I said.

"Killers do things like that," Susan said. "These people seem quite contained."

"They are very professional," I said. "On the other hand, so am I."

"I'm counting on it," Susan said. "And they did seem quite careful to make the explosive charge small and very local, so it would kill only you."

"Also true," I said.

"They'll kill," she said. "But not carelessly."

"If they need to," I said.

"You're like that," she said. "You've killed people."

"When I've had to," I said.

"And you're careful," she said.

"I am," I said.

"They probably think they have to," Susan said.

"In a good cause?" I said.

"Maybe," Susan said.

"Hitler probably thought that he was acting in a good cause."

"And he was wrong," Susan said. "I'm just saying there's some reason, perhaps, to think they may be acting on behalf of a cause they believe in."

"Instead of just greed, or hatred."

"There may be much of that, but maybe they are able to sort of camouflage those impulses with the colors of a high-minded cause."

"Like a foundation or something?" I said. "Say the Herzberg Foundation?"

"Maybe," Susan said.

"For a Harvard Ph.D., you're pretty smart," I said.

She nodded and sipped from her wineglass.

"You and I," she said, "have something few people ever get. And we've worked our asses off to get it."

"I know."

"I couldn't bear it if they killed you," she said.

I grinned at her.

"Me, either," I said.

42

There was a big farmer porch on the front of the house that Ashton Prince had shared with Rosalind Wellington. There was a big tree in the front yard. If it had leaves, I might have known what kind it was. But in winter, with snow on all the limbs and no birds singing, I knew only that it was a tree and would probably have offered swell shade for the porch in summer.

It was a cold morning, and spitting snow. I ate in my car with the engine running and the heater on. The exhaust vapors would have alerted me or anyone like me to the presence of someone in the car. But Rosalind was not anyone like me, and was so self-absorbed that I thought it possible that she was never really alert to anything.

She came out her front door about nine-thirty wearing a

striped multicolored knit cap pulled down over her ears and a bulky black quilted coat that reached her ankles. She paid neither my exhaust vapors nor me any heed at all, and strode off toward the college six blocks away.

When she was gone I took a small gym bag of tools and went to her front door. She hadn't locked it with a key when she came out, so if it was locked, it would be a spring bolt and not a deadbolt. I took out a little flashlight and looked at the door latch. The door didn't close snugly, and I could see the tongue of the spring bolt. Made duck soup look difficult. I took a small putty knife with a flexible blade from my gym bag and slid it into the opening. It took me less than a minute to lever the bolt back and open the door. I put my flashlight and putty knife back in the gym bag, zipped it up, and put it down just inside the front door. I took my jacket off and hung it on the inside doorknob. Spenser, King of the Burglars. B&E our specialty.

In the movies, when somebody searches a home, the place always looks like a model room in Bloomingdale's furniture department. In the actual detective business, sometimes they don't. Rosalind's house was dusty. The living-room rug was threadbare, and the living-room furniture was inexpensive, and some of it sagged. There were dirty dishes in the sink. In the bedroom, the bed wasn't made, and there were a lot of clothes on the floor.

I'd seen worse. I'd tossed a lot of homes.

I had already been there for a while when I came to what must have been Prince's office. It had the feel of a place that had been closed up and silent for a while. The furniture needed help, and the room was dusty. But it was orderly. Prince's desk was neat. To the right of his desk was a big painting of *Lady with a Finch* in a very ordinary-looking black frame. I walked over and looked at it. It had to be a copy, but even so, it was luminous. The tangibility of the lady and the bird was insistent. *The felt surface of life,* I thought.

On the desk, its top closed, was Prince's laptop computer. I didn't need to bother with it. Healy's people would have gone through that and inventoried it after Prince's death. I could get it from Healy. Besides, it was different from the one I had, and I wasn't sure I knew how to make it go.

Prince's calendar pad was open to the month he died, with entries for appointments he never kept scribbled in for dates well after his death. There was a sadness in the gap between the happy assumption that he'd be around to keep those appointments and the fact that he wasn't.

I went through the calendar pad. I got nothing for my trouble. I understood what "pick up suit in a.m." meant. But I didn't care. There was a corkboard on the wall above Prince's desk. There were various notes on it. Some were about scholarly stuff, names of articles, clippings from magazines I never heard of, and on the back of an envelope that had been torn in half was the name Herzberg. And a phone number. I put the note in my shirt pocket.

It took me another two hours to finish the house. Before I left I took one last slow walk through the place. Something kept poking at the edge of my awareness. I finished my final sweep of the house standing just inside the door of Prince's office and slowly surveyed the room. One whole wall was books in a tired-looking bookcase. The window on the opposite wall looked out at the winter barren backyard. The Hermenszoon painting remained hanging on the wall, and then I realized what was bothering me. Except for the copy of *Lady with a Finch,* there were no paintings. In the home of a man who apparently had devoted his adult life to the study and appreciation of paintings, there was only one. The Hermenszoon copy was it.

It was hardly a eureka moment. But it was odd.

43

I went back to my office and called the number I had found on Prince's corkboard. A recording answered. A woman's voice.

"This is the Herzberg Foundation. We can't take your call, but please leave us a message at the sound of the tone."

"Succinct," I said aloud.

Nothing in my office responded.

I called the number every hour for the rest of the afternoon and got the same message. So, at twenty minutes to seven, I shut off the lights, locked up the office, and with my gun in hand, held inconspicuously against my thigh, went down to the alley where I parked. I stopped in the doorway. With my left hand I took out my car keys and, shielded in the doorway, reached out and started my car with the remote.

The car did not explode. Encouraged, I walked down to it, got in, and drove to Cambridge.

When I got to Susan's place and got past the five minutes of Pearl leaping up and lapping and chewing on one of her toys, I went on into the dining area, where Susan had the table set. Tablecloth, good china, nice crystal, a bouquet of flowers in the center, flanked by candles.

I kissed her.

"What's for supper?" I said.

"I've ordered pizza," she said.

"Pizza?"

"You love pizza," Susan said.

"I do," I said. "But the table's set for duck à l'orange."

"Doesn't it look pretty?"

"Suze," I said. "Pizza is normally eaten from the box, standing up, at the kitchen counter."

"I got the flowers in the square," she said. "I think it completes the table."

"It certainly does," I said.

The doorbell rang. Pearl barked.

Susan said, "Make us a drink. I'll get the pizza."

"I'll come with you," I said.

"There's—Oh," she said, "of course."

The three of us went down to the front door, Pearl barking steadily. I had my gun out and stood just to the side, where I could see through the etched-glass window in the door.

It looked like a pizza delivery guy.

"Open the box," I said to him. "I want a look."

He glanced at me with a look that said, "You meet all kinds in Cambridge." But he opened the box, and there was a very large pizza. With mushrooms and peppers.

"Thanks," I said.

Susan paid him and took the pizza while keeping her leg between Pearl and the door's opening. Pearl kept barking. But it was just her usual "Hey, who's that?" bark. I locked and bolted the front door. The pizza guy got back in his car and drove away.

Another hair's-breadth escape.

44

Susan managed to serve the pizza as if it deserved the good china. She had some white wine with hers. I had beer. Old school. Susan took a barely measurable bite off the very end of a slice and chewed it carefully. Then she sipped her wine and put the glass down. I often had trouble putting the glass down.

"I acquired Ashton Prince's doctoral dissertation," she said, "from the BU library."

I drank some beer.

"It's about *Lady with a Finch*," she said.

"How long?"

"One hundred and seventy-three pages."

"About one painting?" I said.

"Oh, don't pretend to be boorish," she said.

"Oh, good," I said. "You think it's pretense."

"You know there is much to say about a great painting, just as there is about a great poem."

"Anyone done one hundred and seventy-three pages on *Sonnet Seventy-three?*" I said.

She smiled.

"Probably," Susan said. "It is difficult to imagine a topic too small, or too silly, for a doctoral dissertation."

"So," I said. "He like the painting?"

"Yes," Susan said. "But that's not really the thrust of the dissertation. It traces the history of the painting, as artifact, from Hermenszoon on."

"Really?"

"Or at least to the time when the dissertation was written."

"Did he trace it to the Hammond?" I said.

"No," Susan said. "At the time he finished the dissertation, the painting was still missing."

"Where did he last locate it?"

"In the possession of someone named Amos Prinz, who had been in the camps with the only surviving member of the Herzberg family. Judah Herzberg looked out for his son Isaac, and for Amos Prinz, who was fourteen when he was sent to the camp, and already orphaned. Isaac was nine when he arrived at Auschwitz."

She paused and drank some wine. And swallowed it slowly and shook her head.

"Nine years old," she said. "My God."

"I've always claimed," I said, "that if I could think of it, someone would do it. But I don't know; I'm not sure I could have thought of the Holocaust."

"I know," Susan said. "Should I go on? Or is it too boring."

I waited until I had chewed and swallowed the large bite of pizza I had taken. Then I said, "It's not boring."

"Okay," she said. "So after a while Judah dies, and Prinz takes over the care of Isaac, you know, sort of like a big brother. They both survived, and when they were liberated, Amos took Isaac back to Amsterdam, where the family had lived. The house had been looted and was boarded up, but Isaac found the painting in a secret place he remembered. His family had hidden it there when the Nazis came."

"Probably the most valuable thing they owned," I said. "What happens next."

"They sold it," Susan said. "Two kids, about fourteen and eighteen by then, destitute. They sold it to an art dealer in Rotterdam for . . . I think he calls it 'a pittance.' And where it went after that, the dissertation doesn't know."

"Do we know the name of the art dealer?"

"No," Susan said. "But I thought it a fascinating story, especially for a doctoral dissertation."

"It's more fascinating than you know," I said. "Did Prince offer any further identification of Amos Prinz?

"No," Susan said. "He says that both Prinz and Herzberg disappeared, as he puts it, 'obscured by the fog of historical events.'"

I nodded and ate some more pizza, and drank some beer, and gave Pearl a crust.

"You know we don't feed her from the table," Susan said.

"Of course we don't," I said.

"It just encourages her to beg."

"What could I have been thinking?" I said.

"Your capacity for tough love gets very low scores," she said.

"Always has," I said.

"However," she said, "your capacity for other kinds may have retired the trophy."

"Pizza," I said, "beer, and you. This is the trophy."

"So how much more fascinating is it?" Susan said.

"Ashton Prince is Jewish, like you," I said. "His real name is Ascher Prinz. His father was at Auschwitz."

"His father?" Susan said.

"I found a phone number and the name Herzberg on a note tacked to the corkboard in his home office."

"Did you call the number?"

"I did," I said. "The answering machine said that it was something called the Herzberg Foundation."

"Did you leave a message?"

"No."

"Did you ever get a live person?"

"No."

"Did you call the phone company?"

"Yeah," I said. "It's a nonpublished number."

"So they wouldn't give you an address," Susan said.

"No."

"But you can find a way to get it," she said.

"Quirk or Healy," I said.

We were quiet.

"You think it's the same people that Prince wrote about in his dissertation," she said.

"Yes."

"You think he's Amos Prinz's son," she said.

"Yes."

"That would be how he would know the things in the dissertation."

"I'd say so."

"So what does it all mean?"

"I don't know," I said. "Yet."

"If he was guilty of some kind of criminal behavior," Susan said, "or even if he just wanted to conceal his identity, wasn't it foolhardy to get that close to it all in his dissertation."

"Maybe," I said.

"Or maybe," Susan said, "he had to write a dissertation, and that's what he had."

"Maybe."

"Or maybe he felt some need to sort of confess," Susan said. "In which case, where better than a dissertation?"

"Your secret will be safe?" I said.

Susan smiled.

"Yes," she said. "I think mine went from my typewriter direct to university microfilms, unseen by human eye."

"You mind that?" I said.

Susan grinned at me.

"I was grateful," she said.

"Bad?"

"It took me two weeks to write it," she said.

"But it got you the Ph.D.," I said.

"That's what it was for," she said.

45

I called Healy in the morning. He said he'd get back to me. I hung up and sat at my computer and typed up a report of what I knew, how I knew it, and what I made of it. I printed out two copies, put them in self-sealing envelopes, put first-class stamps on them, and walked to the end of my hall, where there was a mail chute. Healy called back in less than an hour.

"Phone number is listed on Market Street in Brighton," he said.

"Pays to be a state police captain," I said.

"Not in real money," Healy said.

He gave me the address.

"You want to tell me more?" he said.

"I just sent you a letter, and a copy to Belson," I said.

"Quirk's man?"

"Yeah," I said.

"I talked with him yesterday," Healy said. "He filled me in on the bomb."

"I have written down everything I know, and everything I suspect, and how I know it, and why I suspect it. I reread the thing before I mailed it, and it's beautifully written."

"In case they win and you lose?"

"Expect the best," I said. "Plan for the worst."

"Well, at least I'll have a keepsake," Healy said.

"That doesn't sound like a vote of confidence," I said.

"They seem to know what they're doing," Healy said.

"And they've missed me twice."

"If you hadn't had the dog the first time. If you hadn't thrown your bag the second time," Healy said. "You're alive mostly through luck."

"'Luck is the residue of design,'" I said.

"You quoting somebody again?"

"Branch Rickey," I said.

"Jesus," Healy said. "You know stuff most people don't even care about. You going to go visit the Herzberg Foundation?"

"Yep."

"Belson told me about your lure theory."

"Nothing wrong with it," I said. "It's a way to keep contact with them. We lose that and we got nothing."

"Did you like this guy Prince?" Healy said.

"Hell, no," I said.

"But you're willing to die to catch his murderers."

"I'm not willing to die," I said. "I'm willing to risk it. I was supposed to keep him alive."

"I know," Healy said. "I know. How's Susan feel about it?"

"She doesn't like it, either," I said. "But she knows I need to do this."

"She understands?" Healy said.

"Yes."

"Most women don't."

"Susan's not most women," I said.

"No," Healy said. "She certainly isn't."

We hung up.

46

made some fresh coffee and poured myself a cup and sat at
my desk and sipped it. I kept my right-hand top drawer
open in my desk so I could reach the .357 Mag in case of
emergency. I brought my memo up on the computer screen
and read it again. It was a surprising amount of information
when you looked at it listed there. Proving anything was
maybe an issue. I could go over to the Herzberg Foundation
in Brighton and see what was shaking there. I could go talk
to Lloyd the Lawyer, see if I could pry loose any information on the Herzberg Foundation, which I could then take
with me when I went over there to see what was shaking.
Normally you don't get much out of lawyers, but maybe if
Mort the Tort understood that he was sitting on at least two
murders and two attempted, he might loosen up a little.

My office door opened. I put my hand on the .357. Quirk came in. I took my hand off the .357.

"You look like you just had a date with Renée Zellweger and things went well," I said.

Quirk smiled, which was not common for Quirk. He got some coffee from the fresh pot and sat in one of my client chairs.

"Good news and bad news," Quirk said. "Bad news: the plates on that Lexus were stolen, so we got nothing there. Good news . . ."

He smiled again. Twice in the same morning. He must have been ecstatic.

"We traced the tattooed ID numbers," he said.

"So the hell with the Lexus," I said.

"Went through the Holocaust Museum," Quirk said, "in D.C. Epstein was helpful; got an agent to go over from FBI headquarters. They told us about a place in Germany where they keep a huge collection of Nazi stuff. We got hold of the American embassy. Needed a senator and two congressmen to do it, but we got them to send somebody up there, and she said that there were something like five hundred three-ring notebooks filled with names and tattooed ID numbers of everybody that was in Auschwitz. Every prisoner."

"Imagine keeping track," I said.

"Imagine," Quirk said.

"And who had our tattoo?" I said.

"Fella named Judah Herzberg."

"Hot dog!" I said.

"Listed as deceased," Quirk said, "and a date: August 1943."

"The people who've been trying to ace me must be part of something to do with him," I said.

"How 'bout the Herzberg Foundation?"

"Yeah," I said. "Them. I sent a memo to Healy this morning, copy to Belson. Lemme print it out."

Quirk must have exhausted himself, smiling twice. He sat silently as I printed out the memo and handed it to him. He read it. And nodded when he finished.

"Amos Prinz," he said.

"Uh-huh."

"In Auschwitz with Judah Herzberg," he said. "And he stole the picture, and sixty years later his son is involved in the theft and attempted retrieval of the same painting."

"Uh-huh."

"So where does the Herzberg Foundation fit in?" Quirk said.

"I don't know. Getting the painting back? Maybe. Revenge? Maybe. Justice or something? Maybe."

"Think they're the ones tried to kill you?"

"Yes."

"You got an address for them?" Quirk said.

"Yep."

"You thinking about going over there," Quirk said. "Ask them this?"

"I am."

"Good," Quirk said. "We both know if I show up, or Healy, these people will disperse like the morning mist."

"How poetic."

"Fuck poetic," Quirk said. "We need to hang on to them until we can connect enough dots to arrest them."

"For what, exactly," I said.

"Somebody killed Prince," Quirk said. "And your building super."

"And you're sure it was the Herzberg Foundation?" I said.

"That's one of the dots," Quirk said. "You got something better?"

"No," I said. "I think you're right."

"You got fewer rules to follow," Quirk said. "Just don't scare them off."

"And what if they attempt to kill me?" I said.

"Try to avoid that," Quirk said. "At least until you've found something we can use."

"Not only poetic," I said, "but sentimental, too."

"You gonna do it or not," Quirk said.

"Sure," I said.

47

I was back in the Hammond Museum. In the director's office. Looking at the bare branches through the window, and talking to Richards, the director.

"I am sympathetic, Mr. Spenser, and I appreciate the integrity of returning our check because you felt you hadn't done the job well enough."

"I'm hired to protect a guy and he gets killed," I said. "How much worse could I have done it?"

"Several of the policemen we've talked with said there was nothing you could have done, given the setup."

"I could have prevented him from walking into the setup," I said.

Richards nodded and smiled.

"What can I do for you?" he said.

"Have you ever had any requests to sell *Lady with a Finch?*"

"Recently?" he said.

"Ever?" I said.

"Oh, of course. There are private collectors who are quite passionate in their desire for one or another piece of art."

"Do you have a record of the offers," I said.

"We probably have a file somewhere," Richards said. "I can't really say."

"Is there someone who could say?"

"We preserve and display art," Richards said. "We're not in the business of selling it."

I nodded.

"Anybody named Herzberg?" I said.

Richards frowned.

"I'm not really comfortable," he said, "talking to you without our attorney."

I shook my head.

"Look, Mr. Richards," I said. "I am not a cop. I am self-employed. You can lie to me with impunity. I'm used to it."

"I don't wish to lie to you," he said.

"Whether you do or don't," I said, "talking with me doesn't require a lawyer."

Richards nodded. He shifted a little in his chair and stared for a moment out the window. Behind the museum, the snow was still clean and looked relatively fresh.

"Herzberg is the name of a former owner of *Lady with a Finch*," he said. "A wealthy Dutch Jew who died in one of the Nazi death camps during the Second World War. *Lady with a Finch* was confiscated by the Nazis."

"Where did you get it?" I said.

"It was donated to the museum, in his will, by a long-time patron of the museum named Wendell Forbes," Richards said.

"Where did he get it?" I said.

"He told us that it was purchased from a dealer in Brussels," Richards said.

"Is there a way to trace it back?" I said.

"You mean past ownership?"

"Yeah."

"You'd have to talk with the Forbes estate about that," Richards said.

"That's an exciting prospect," I said. "Is any of the family around?"

"All of this is before my time," Richards said. "I don't really know. Apparently, Wendell Forbes was the only one interested in art."

"Okay," I said. "Tell me a little about Morton Lloyd."

"Morton Lloyd?"

"Yeah," I said. "I'm interested in everything."

"He's our attorney," Richards said. "I believe you met him earlier."

"I did," I said. "How did he come to represent you?"

"He's a member of our board," Richards said.

"So he works pro bono?" I said.

Richards smiled faintly.

"We pay him a retainer for general consultation," Richards said. "And if there's billable work to be done, he does it at cost."

"He says."

Richards smiled but didn't comment.

"And it was he who suggested you use Ashton Prince in regard to the stolen painting," I said.

"Yes," Richards said.

"Did he say how he knew Prince?"

"I don't recall that he did," Richards said.

"And no one has consulted you about the painting in any way since Prince's death?"

Richards looked genuinely startled.

"I am under the impression that the painting no longer exists," he said.

"And you have no reason to doubt that?" I said.

"I wish I did," Richards said. "Do you think it is not destroyed?"

"Don't know," I said. "But I'd bet it wasn't."

"That would be wonderful news," Richards said. "Art is always one of a kind. If it's gone, it cannot be replaced."

"So no one has contacted you in any way about the painting?"

"No."

"I find out something," I said, "I'll let you know."

"Thank you," Richards said. "Have I been of any help?"

"Not much," I said.

"I'm sorry," Richards said.

"Don't feel bad," I said. "Nobody else has been much help, either."

48

Morton Lloyd did business out of an old gray stone building on Batterymarch. His office itself was aggressively colonial, right down to the receptionist, who looked a bit like Molly Pitcher. There were prints of American militia companies on the paneled walls. And a big painting of Cornwallis's surrender. The painting looked amateurish to me.

"My name is Spenser," I said to the receptionist. "I need to consult with Mr. Lloyd."

"Mr. Lloyd is with a client," she said. "Do you have an appointment."

"I can wait," I said.

"You didn't say if you had an appointment, sir."

"Everyone has an appointment, ma'am, sooner, or later, in Samarra."

"What?" Molly Pitcher said.

"I don't have an appointment," I said. "But I have nothing else to do today. And I may as well do it here. Tell Mr. Lloyd it is in regard to *Lady with a Finch.*"

"Lady what?" Molly said.

"He'll understand," I said. *"Lady with a Finch."*

She wrote it down on a small pad of paper. I smiled. She looked at me without smiling.

"Come on," I said. "My smile is infectious. Everyone says so. No one can resist smiling back."

She looked at me as if I were a talking baboon and flashed me an entirely mechanical smile, and turned back to her computer. I sat down in a black captain's chair with an eagle in flight stenciled in gold on the back. It was very quiet in the reception area. A couple of times Molly Pitcher looked half surreptitiously up from her computer, and each time I gave her my most winsome smile. And each time she had no reaction beyond going back to her computer. She must have been a woman of iron self-control.

The door to the inner office opened, and Mort the Tort ushered out a middle-aged couple.

"So just sit tight," he was saying. "I'm sure we can settle this without going to court."

He walked them past me to the outer door, opened it for them, and closed it after they'd left. Then he turned quite deliberately and looked at me.

"What the hell do you want?" he said.

I stood.

"Thanks, Mort," I said. "I would like to come in and chat."

Molly Pitcher piped up.

"He says it's about"—she looked at her note—"a lady and a finch."

I smiled at Lloyd.

"Close enough," I said.

Lloyd jerked his head at me and went into his office. I followed him. He closed the door behind me and went around and sat at his big Ipswich maple desk.

"Okay," he said. "What is it?"

The inner office had a fireplace with a big wooden sign over it that read *Paul Revere, Silversmith.* It looked as if it had been manufactured in China in 2008. A harpoon leaned in one corner.

I sat down.

"I need what you can tell me about you and Ashton Prince and the Herzberg Foundation," I said.

"You come here and bother me about that?" Lloyd said. "I am busy. I have another client in five minutes. I have others after him. I don't have time for your cockamamie ideas."

"You're a lot deeper into a mess than you want to be," I said. "This has turned into two murders, two attempted murders, a bomb, and, of course, the priceless painting."

Lloyd stared at me.

"I know you offered to represent Prince against Walford University," I said. "I know you suggested him to broker the deal to get the painting back. I know you represent the

Herzberg Foundation, and that you allow them to drive at least one car registered to you. I know that you represent them pro bono, which is not your style."

"I'm Jewish," Lloyd said.

"So?"

"It's a Jewish organization, for God's sake," Lloyd said. "I have several cars. I donated one to them."

"In what way is it a Jewish organization?" I said.

"It is concerned with the Holocaust."

"How?" I said.

"Restoring the historical record," he said. "If you're not Jewish, you cannot understand the full meaning of the Holocaust."

"Probably not," I said. "Did you know that Ashton Prince's real name was Ascher Prinz, and that his father, Amos, was in Auschwitz with Judah and Isaac Herzberg?"

"No."

"Do you think the Herzberg Foundation is related to Judah and Isaac?" I said.

"How would I know," he said.

"Are they interested in maybe recovering *Lady with a Finch*?"

"That is privileged information," Lloyd said.

"We'll put this all together sooner or later," I said. "And if there's bad news about you, it'll go easier if we got it from you."

"You're not a cop," he said.

"True," I said. "But I know one."

His hands were resting on his expensive desk. He looked down at them. Then he cleared his throat and shook his head.

"I have nothing further to say."

I nodded and took one of my business cards out of my shirt pocket.

"This whole thing is going to go right out from underneath you pretty soon. And if you're still hanging on, it'll take you down with it."

He was still looking at the backs of his hands.

"We have nothing left to discuss," he said.

I stood.

"I'll let myself out," I said, and walked to the door.

As I opened it, I looked back and nodded at my card on his desk.

"Don't lose the card," I said.

49

Brighton is mostly middle-class residential, and the house on Market Street fit in nicely. It had white aluminum siding and a porch across the front enclosed with jalousie windows. The concrete sidewalk was neatly shoveled, and ice melt had been scattered on it, and on the two steps to the porch door. A white signpost stood beside the door, with a white wooden sign hanging from it that read in black letters:

HERZBERG FOUNDATION
ART AND JUSTICE

I opened the porch door and went in. On the inside front door was a small brass sign that said *Office*. I opened that door and I was in what must have once been a living room but was now a reception area with a desk and several chairs, in case you needed to wait. At the desk was the guy I had seen with Missy at the Walford library.

"What can I do for you?" he said.

"You are?" I said.

"Ariel Herzberg," he said. "And you?"

"Call me Ishmael," I said. "Your father was Isaac Herzberg."

Herzberg pushed his swivel chair away from the desk and leaned as far back in the chair as the spring would allow and stared at me.

"Your grandfather was Judah Herzberg," I said. "He died in Auschwitz. Isaac, your father, survived Auschwitz and was liberated by the Russians with his friend Amos Prinz in 1945. He was about fourteen at the time. Amos was about eighteen."

"He would have pronounced it 'Ah-mose,'" Ariel said.

"They went together to Amsterdam," I said. "Recovered a painting from a secret room in the now-abandoned Herzberg home, took it to Rotterdam and sold it to an art dealer for much less than it was worth but enough to feed them for a while."

"So?" Ariel said after a bit.

"The painting was *Lady with a Finch*," I said. "It was stolen a little while back, from the Hammond Museum."

"I read about that," Ariel said.

"I think you stole it," I said.

"And of course you have evidence."

"I think you blew up Ashton Prince," I said.

"Evidence?"

"I think you tried twice to kill me, and succeeded in killing a guy named Francisco," I said.

"Evidence?" Ariel said again.

"Ah," I said. "There's the rub."

"It is a big rub," Ariel said. "Don't you think?"

"It is," I said. "But I'm working on it. Did you know that Ashton Prince is the son of Amos Prinz?"

"I know nothing except what I have read in the papers."

"Do you know—"

I stopped. I was going to ask if he knew Missy Minor, and if he knew Morton Lloyd, and what relationship he had with either. But if he'd tried twice to kill me for investigating, what might he do with a potential witness?

"You had a question?" Ariel said.

He would admit nothing, anyway. Why put them in jeopardy?

"I decided not to ask it," I said.

"America is a great country," he said. "We are free to do what we will."

I had already baited him as much as I needed to. He knew what I knew. If it was as dangerous to him as I thought it was, maybe he'd make a run at me, and I could catch him at it. I took a business card from my shirt pocket. On the back I wrote his grandfather's death camp number, and handed him the card.

"What is this number?" he said.

"Judah Herzberg's Auschwitz ID number," I said. "You probably have it tattooed on your arm."

"You appear a good investigator," Ariel said.

"Stalwart, too," I said.

"No doubt," Ariel said. "No doubt."

He must have pressed a button someplace, because a door opened behind him and a big muscular blond guy came in wearing a tight T-shirt and looking scary. He paused beside Ariel's desk and looked at him. I could see that there were numbers tattooed on his forearm.

"Throw Mr. Spenser out, Kurt," Ariel said to him. "Not gently."

50

Kurt studied me for a moment. We were about the same size, but he didn't seem daunted. I speculated that they were trying to get me to draw my gun so they could shoot me and claim self-defense. It didn't matter. I wasn't going to draw my gun. My frustration content was saturating. I needed to hit somebody, and Kurt looked good for it.

Kurt shuffled toward me with his left foot forward and his hands held loosely up on either side of his head. So he had some idea what he was doing. On the other hand, I did, too, and I'd been doing it longer. He swung his right leg up and across in a martial arts–type kick. I stepped inside it, close to him, so not much of the kick got me, and hit him in the throat with the crotch between the thumb and forefinger of my right hand. The guy who taught me the punch called it "the tiger's claw." Kurt grunted and spun away from me, and settled back into his stance. Some people fell down when I hit them that way. I slid toward him with a left jab, which landed well, and a right cross, which landed even better. Kurt bobbed and wove a little and hit me on the chin with the heel of his right hand. It backed me up a couple of steps, and he came after me. I blocked a left and then a right, and feinted a straight left to his face. He brought his right arm across to block it, and I looped a big left hook over the block and nailed him on the right cheekbone. He staggered. That was encouraging. But he didn't go down.

I followed with a right uppercut, which would have ended it, but he leaned away from it and it missed. My right side was exposed, and Kurt hammered a solid left hook into my ribs. I turned with the punch so I was at right angles to him and came around with my right elbow and hit him in the temple. He staggered again, and I heard his breath exhale in a kind of snort. I had him if I was quick. I went with the flow and followed the right elbow with the left forearm, then a left back fist and a right cross. All in rhythm. Everything was loose now and warm and moving as it should. I hit him with a left hook to the body, right hook to the body. He stumbled backward. I stayed on him. Left to the body, right to the body. His hands dropped. Left hook to the head. Right hook to the head. His hands were hanging at his sides now. It was like hitting the heavy bag. I jabbed him again in the face, and then turned my hip and brought the right uppercut that had missed before. He was too far gone to slip it this time, and it caught him square. He took another step backward. His legs gave out. And he sat suddenly on the floor, and his eyes rolled back in his head.

My hands hurt.

I looked at Ariel Herzberg.

"You think they'll put my statue outside the Museum of Fine Arts?" I said.

"Kurt is good," Ariel said. "Which means you're very good."

"Keep it in mind," I said.

"It is a temporary triumph," he said. "Enjoy it while you can."

I walked to his desk and took hold of his nose and sort of shook his head for him.

"So far, I like my chances better than yours," I said.

And I left.

51

We hadn't had a big, serious snowstorm all winter. It had snowed moderately, and often, and it was doing it again. The cumulative effect of moderate and often was pretty much the same as big, serious. The snow was steady but not dense, and the flakes were small. But it was enough to cover up the compacted dirty snow that had preceded it, and for a little while the city would look clean again.

I walked up Berkeley Street wearing my plaid longshoreman's cap and a fleece-lined leather jacket. Because I had the jacket zipped up, and people were seeking to do me ill, I had taken my gun off my belt and put it in my side pocket. I also looked around a lot. At Columbus I turned right and went in the big arched door of Shawmut Insurance Company and rode up in the black iron elevator to see Winifred Minor.

She was in the same office I'd seen her in before. The door was open. I knocked on the outer edge of the door opening and stepped in. She looked up at me and saw who it was and stiffened and looked at me some more without speaking. I sat down.

"Hi," I said.

She continued to look at me silently.

"You never finished your lunch," I said.

She didn't say anything.

"How 'bout that snow?" I said.

Silence.

"If you don't like the weather in New England, wait a minute," I said.

She looked down at her desk.

"Everybody talks about the weather," I said. "But nobody does anything about it."

She looked up from her desk.

"All right," she said. "Enough. I'll talk to you. What do you want?"

"Thank God," I said. "I was almost down to singing 'Stormy Weather.'"

She almost smiled.

"At least I escaped that," she said. "What do you want?"

"Know a man named Ariel Herzberg?" I said.

"No."

"Your daughter does," I said.

"So?"

"I saw him visiting her at Walford last week," I said.

"So?"

"He's killed two people that I know of, and tried twice, so far, to kill me."

She kept looking at me, and her breathing became harder, as if she was short of breath.

"If she's involved with a man like that . . ." I said.

"Who did he kill," Winifred asked.

Her voice was raspy.

"He killed Ashton Prince," I said. "And the superintendent in my building. Super's name was Francisco Cabrera."

"Was that part of the attempt to kill you?"

"Yes."

"Did the super interrupt them?" she said.

"No," I said. "They interrupted him. Apparently they rang the bell. When he answered, they put a gun on him and forced him to open my door. Then they took him to the cellar and shot him in the head."

"Did Ariel do this himself?"

"Probably not," I said. "He probably had people do it for him."

"And you've seen her with him?"

"Missy," I said. "Yes."

"And you assume they're involved."

"They were people who knew each other," I said.

"Is there anything I could say . . . or do . . . to make you leave this alone?"

"I don't think so," I said.

"You have an office just down the street," she said.

"Yes."

"Let's go there to talk," she said.

"Okay."

52

'd given her some coffee, and she was sitting in a client chair with her legs crossed, sipping it. Her knees were good-looking. She looked past me for a time, out my window, where the small snowflakes fell. They were well spaced and in no great hurry. She didn't seem to be in much of a hurry herself. That was okay. She hadn't come here to drink coffee and look at the snow.

I was behind my desk. In my Aeron chair. With the right-hand top drawer of my desk open, and a cup of fresh coffee in my hand. I drank some. And looked at her knees. And waited.

After a little while she shifted her gaze from the snowfall to me.

"When I was with the Bureau," she said, "before Missy

was born, I was young, single, and ferocious. I was going to prove something. I was going to be the best goddamned agent since Melvin Purvis."

"That's the spirit," I said.

"I know," she said. "Seems kind of, what? Pathetic, now all this time later. What we know about the Bureau. What we know about the government. What we know about . . ." She shrugged. "What we know about everything."

"We all gotta forgive ourselves our youth," I said.

"But it was kind of pathetic," she said. "Doesn't it sound pathetic?"

"Yeah," I said. "Some."

She looked relieved, as if I'd complimented her.

"I was in Chicago," she said. "And we were working on a case involving art theft from a private collector in Evanston."

"Where Northwestern is," I said. Just to let her know I was alert.

"Yuh. There were several of us on it; the guy they were stolen from was connected in D.C. I was the only female, and I outworked all of them. We always had a lot of money to pay for information. Local cops resented us for that."

"They never had enough," I said.

"No. I got a lead from a snitch, I don't even remember the details. They may have tried to recruit him for something. He told me about a gang of art thieves that he said had something to do with the World War Two prisons or something, and how a lot of Jews got killed."

She paused and drank some coffee and smiled very slightly.

"He told me all this like it was news. I don't think he'd ever heard of the Holocaust and was only vaguely aware of World War Two."

"Snitches don't always have a broad historical perspective," I said.

"Probably why they're snitches," she said. "Anyway, the tip was good. It led me to a guy who was apparently in the business of finding and liberating Jewish-owned art stolen by the Nazis."

"Still?" I said.

"Well, we're talking twenty years ago," she said. "But yes, still."

"Holocaust throws a long shadow," I said. "Doesn't it."

"Yes. So I confront this guy, and he's, like, unshakeable. Doesn't deny. Doesn't admit. And is so charming about it," she said. "I spent a lot of time with him, working on him. But more and more I was spending it because I wanted to. I started looking forward to seeing him again. And I could tell, I thought, that he felt the same way."

"Until one day . . ." I said.

"Yeah," she said. "In a room at the Park Hyatt near the water tower off Michigan Avenue."

"I know where it is," I said.

"It became our place," she said. "We didn't go there all the time. We couldn't afford it. But on special dates. You know, our one-week anniversary. Our one-month anniversary . . ."

She stopped talking for a bit and looked through my window at the soft snow.

"Pathetic," she said.

"No," I said. "A run like that isn't pathetic. It may be ill-advised. Might even be contrived. Might be cathexis and not love. But the feelings are real when you have them. And they are not valueless."

"'Cathexis'?"

"Libidinal energy," I said. "Sorry. I'm in love with a shrink."

"And it's different than love?"

"The shrink I'm in love with says so."

"I wonder how much shrinks know about love?" she said.

"Mine knows a lot," I said. "But not, I think, because she's a shrink. How soon did you get pregnant?"

"You know where this is going," she said.

"I think so."

"Maybe you and I are developing some cathexis?" she said.

"Absolutely," I said. "But my shrink won't let me."

"I was pregnant the second month we were together," she said.

"I assume the investigation had slowed during this period."

"Worse," she said. "I warned him what we had."

"How'd he take to the pregnancy?" I said.

"He wanted me to abort," she said.

"And?"

She shook her head.

"I had already sold out the Bureau for him," she said. "I couldn't . . . I couldn't kill the baby for him."

"How'd he take that?"

"He said there were things he had to do, and they didn't include marriage and children."

"He have numbers tattooed on his forearm?"

"Yes."

"The baby was Missy?"

"Yes."

"And the father was Ariel Herzberg," I said.

"Yes," she said.

53

Her eyes had filled with tears. I handed her a box of Kleenex and took her coffee cup and poured her some fresh coffee. I looked at my watch; it was two in the afternoon. Late enough in the day. I took a bottle of Irish whiskey from a drawer in my file cabinet and held it up. She stared blankly at it for a moment, then nodded. I poured some into the coffee and gave her back her cup.

"You had the baby alone," I said.

She sipped her enhanced coffee.

"Yes," she said. "I obviously couldn't let the Bureau know what was going on. So I took a leave. My doctor, a lovely woman named Martha Weidhaus, contrived me a medical reason. I had the baby, hired a nanny, and went back to work."

"Pressed for money?" I said.

"Of course," she said. "Ariel would occasionally send some, for which I was grateful. But I could never count on it."

"Did you see him?"

"No. After I got pregnant he disappeared."

"What does Missy know about him?" I said.

"I told her he was dead," Winifred said. "And she bought that, though she still wanted to know about him, what his name was, what he was like, what he worked at, how we had met. I created quite an admirable fictional character over the years."

"Anyone ask you about that case you had in Chicago?"

"Often," Winifred said. "It kept poking at me with its nose. Like a dog at suppertime. It's one of the reasons I left, and took this job."

"Plus better pay," I said. "And no heavy lifting."

She nodded.

"Missy is seeing Ariel. Does she know who he is?"

"Yes," Winifred said. "He showed up one day when she was sixteen and introduced himself."

"Jesus Christ!"

"It wasn't the way to do it," she said. "And I don't know how much damage it did. But Ariel always wanted what he wanted and didn't think much about damage . . . to others. She got a little hysterical at me for lying to her, at him for not being there, but he talked to her, and I watched her fall in love with him the way I did."

"Why did he show up?"

"I don't know," Winifred said. "I never knew why he sent us money when he did. I never know why he does what he does. But I am almost certain it is finally in his own best interest, not someone else's."

"He hang around for a while?" I said.

"Yes, still does. He and I have not taken up again. I'm older and wiser. But he sees Missy regularly. I have warned her about him. But she is . . . She is infatuated with him . . . like I was. She wanted to be an art major. And she wanted to go to Walford. He got her in. '*No problem,*' he said. 'I have a friend there.'"

"Ashton Prince," I said.

"Yes."

"What do they do together?" I said.

She shook her head and drank some coffee.

"I don't know," she said. "They don't . . . They exclude me."

"That'll fix you," I said.

"For telling her he was dead?"

"Yeah."

"I was trying to protect her," Winifred said. "He's not cruel, or even mean. But he's entirely interested in himself, and what he wants."

"Well," I said. "I'm going to solve that problem for you."

"You have enough evidence?"

"Not yet," I said.

"But you will," Winifred said.

"Sooner or later," I said.

She stared at me for a while and nodded.

"Yes," she said. "You will."

She handed me her cup.

"Don't bother with the coffee," she said.

I poured some whiskey in the cup and gave it back to her. She sipped some.

"I'll be as kind as I can be," I said. "If she's involved, I'll try to keep her, and you, out of it."

"Oh, God," Winifred said. "It will kill her. I don't know what to hope for."

"It's well beyond hope," I said.

"I know," she said, and sipped again. "If I were outside looking in, which I'm not, I wish I were—if I were outside, I'd think this was very interesting."

"Because?" I said.

"Because you're as implacable as he is," she said. "Be interesting to see who wins."

"Yeah," I said. "I'm interested in that, too."

54

An outfit named Galvin Contracting came in and restored my bombed-out bedroom. They put in a new window, changed the lock on my front door, and even assembled the new bed when it was delivered. They repainted the bedroom, same color, more gray than tan but with some hint of both, depending on the light. Susan came with me when I moved back in. She brought with her a bunch of linens that she'd purchased for me. I helped her carry them in.

"How'd you know what color I'd paint it?" I said.

She looked at me and made a sound that, had she been less elegant, would have been a snort.

"Are you implying by that look that I'm boringly predictable?" I said.

She nodded vigorously.

We made the bed together. The sheets and pillowcases were plum-colored. I went to the linen closet in the bathroom and got a black down comforter and put it on the bed. Susan went to the living room and got a large plastic bag with several decorative pillows in it. They appeared to match or contrast with the plum sheets.

"What are those for?" I said.

She ignored me and began to place them strategically on my bed until they covered more than half.

"Where do I sleep?" I said.

"At night you take them off," she said.

"And put them on again in the morning?"

"When you make the bed," she said.

"Every day?" I said.

"Do you make the bed every day?"

"I do," I said.

"Then of course," she said. "Every day."

"Will you be stopping by to inspect every day?" I said.

"No more than usual," she said.

I smiled.

"Do I sense that they may not be on the bed when I'm not here?"

"Hard to predict," I said.

"But they look so beautiful," she said.

There was nowhere to go with that, so I said, "How about lunch?"

"Sounds good to me," she said. "Where?"

"Here," I said. "I'll leave the bedroom door open, and we can admire the pillows while we eat."

Susan looked at me kind of slant-eyed sideways and went to the kitchen counter and sat.

"Whatcha gonna make?" she said.

"How about cold chicken with mixed fruit and whole-wheat biscuits?"

"What could be better," she said.

"Well, there's one thing I can think of," I said. "But there's so many damn pillows on the bed. . . ."

She grinned.

"Oh, shut up," she said.

I took out the chicken to allow the refrigerator chill to dissipate, and some fruit salad, and started mixing the biscuits.

"Is her mother going with you when you talk to Missy?" Susan said.

"No," I said. "Winifred says that she and her daughter are so at odds that she would only make matters worse."

"At odds over the father?" Susan asked.

"I would say so."

"Women fighting over a man," Susan said.

"It's that simple?" I said.

"Oh, God, no," Susan said. "I was just sort of musing aloud. Consider the girl. She thinks she has no father, that he's dead, and she fantasizes the dream father, and then when she's sixteen years old he appears and he seems to be the dream father she had imagined: handsome, mysterious, charming, and he comes to her. She's furious with her mother for denying him all these sixteen years. On the other hand, it took him sixteen years to come see her. Who should she love? Who can she trust? How should she feel?"

"Sixteen years is a long time when you're sixteen," I said.

"A lifetime," Susan said. "Do you have a plan?"

"I thought I'd ask her about her relationship with her father and the Herzberg Foundation."

Susan smiled.

"Subtle," she said.

I shrugged.

"At the beginning I was walking around saying, 'What's going on?' At least now I've narrowed the focus of my general questions."

"And after you've asked?" Susan said.

"I'll listen," I said. "You know how that works."

"I do," she said. "Though my goal is generally somewhat different."

"We're both after the truth," I said.

"There's that," Susan said.

55

fell in beside Missy Minor as she walked near the student union.

"I don't want to talk to you," she said.

"I don't blame you," I said. "You have so much you don't want me to know."

She stopped walking and turned toward me.

"What's that mean?" she said.

It had stopped snowing during the night. But it was kind of cold, and the wind tossed the new snow around in small white eddies.

"I'll explain if we can get out of the cold," I said. "Buy you breakfast?"

"I had breakfast," she said.

"No reason you can't have another one," I said.

"I'll have coffee," she said.

We went into the student union and got a table in the far corner of the cafeteria. At mid-morning, the place was half empty. I had milk and sugar in my coffee. She drank hers black.

"I know that your father is Ariel Herzberg and that you and he see one another," I said.

"My mother tell you that?"

"I've talked with your mother," I said. "But I actually saw you and him together in the library."

"You've been spying on me," she said.

"I have."

"Why," she said. "Why don't you just leave me alone?"

"Wish I could," I said. "But you are alleged to have been intimate with a murder victim, and the man who killed him appears to be your father."

"You're disgusting," she said.

"But only a little," I said. "You involved at all with the foundation?"

"I'm not involved with anything," she said. "I hate you."

Even for nineteen, she was young.

"Must be hard," I said. "No father for sixteen years and all of a sudden a father. What's that like?"

"It's a bitch, is what it's like," she said. "I mean, for sixteen years my mother lied through her teeth that he was dead. You know, she never even told me he sent money. You know that they were never married?"

"She told you they were?"

"Yeah, and that he died after I was conceived," she said. "Fact is, for crissake, she was shacking up with some guy who had no intention of marrying her, and when she got knocked up, he left."

"Tough on her, I guess," I said.

"She wanted him to marry her? There's a laugh. He didn't love her. He was just enjoying a little joyride, you know?"

"But he came back," I said.

"He came back for me," she said. "He said he always wanted to but she wouldn't let him."

"Why do you suppose she did that?" I said.

"Jealousy," she said. "She knew if he was in my life I'd love him, and she didn't want that."

"Wow," I said. "She was pretty mean, huh?"

Nothing like sowing a little family strife for stirring up information.

"Awful," Missy said. "But Daddy is great. He got me into Walford. He introduced me to Ashton, Professor Prince; he's been great."

"Who pays the tuition?" I said.

"She does. She can afford it, already had the money put aside. Besides, she's got a good job."

"Yeah," I said. "I imagine the foundation doesn't pay too much."

"God, no. Daddy's not interested in money."

"What does the foundation do?" I said.

She opened her mouth and closed it. I could almost read her face. *This way danger lay.*

"I don't know," she said.

"That's surprising," I said. "How close you are."

"He loves me, and I love him," she said. "That's all anyone needs to know."

"'Cept me," I said. "I need to know more."

"Well, I'm not going to tell you anything," she said.

She began to cry and stood suddenly and walked away, almost running. In the detective business, charm never fails.

56

With my feet on my desk and the *Globe* open before me, I phoned Susan.

"I see in the paper," I said, "that there's an Evening of Verse being held at a church in Cambridge."

"Hot dog," Susan said.

"One of the performers is Rosalind Wellington."

"No kidding," Susan said.

"Do you remember who Rosalind Wellington is?" I said.

"No."

"She's Mrs. Ashton Prince," I said.

"Uh-huh."

"Want to go?"

" 'Go'?" Susan said.

"Attend, listen to her read her poetry," I said.

"You think she is any good?" Susan said. "That any of the poets reading there will be any good?"

"No," I said. "No, of course not. It'll be awful."

"Wow," Susan said. "That's persuasive."

"So you want to go?" I said.

"No," Susan said. "What I want to know is why you do?"

"Remember you got Prince's Ph.D. dissertation and read it?" I said.

"I do. An act of breathtaking self-sacrifice, may I say."

"We learned a lot from that," I said.

"You're welcome."

"I thought I might learn something from her poetry," I said.

Susan was silent for a moment.

Then she said, "You might. One of the predictable things about the kind of poets you are nearly certain to hear is that their poetry will be about the angst of being them. It will be hideous, but she might actually reveal something useful in the process."

"I'm gonna go," I said.

"You'll have to brave it without me," she said. "I get enough interior angst every day, fifty minutes an hour."

"Okay," I said.

"Not that I don't admire your fortitude," Susan said.

I admired it myself. The event started at seven; I was there at quarter of. The room was barren, with cement walls painted yellow. It looked like it should have been swept more recently than it had been. There were about fifty folding chairs and maybe fifteen people, grouped around a maple table with a lectern on it. The lighting was overhead and harsh. The room was too hot.

I took off my coat and sat. If anyone noticed the gun on my hip, they didn't react. They were too deeply involved, I assumed, in the life of the imagination. They were generally not deeply involved in elegance. At seven, a heavy woman in an ankle-length dress walked in and stood at the lectern and welcomed us to the Evening of Verse. She announced that at the end of the evening, the poems read tonight would be for sale at the back of the room for five dollars.

Then a guy came out and read a detailed description of a series of homosexual acts. In the rhyme scheme, "foreskin" was rhymed with "more sin." And "between us" with "penis."

The next reader was a skinny woman with her hair in a tight bun who wrote about masturbation, then came a guy with a very long braid, who read something. But I couldn't tell what it was about. Sadly, Rosalind Wellington was near the end of the program, and I might have left before she came on if Susan hadn't admired my fortitude. So I stuck it out. When she came on, she was all in black, wearing a hat with a veil.

"'So Little Left Behind,'" she intoned." 'An Ode to My Late Husband.'"

She looked down at the papers on the lectern and began

to read in what she must have thought was a dramatic
monotone.

> *My husband went loudly into the eternal night.*
> *No time to rage, or set things right.*
> *No legacy, though one was promised.*
> *A legacy quite odd,*
> *Two painted ladies like a god.*
> *One true as starlight,*
> *The other one a fraud.*
> *The starlight lady hidden,*
> *The fraud in public view.*
> *As I who've come unbidden*
> *Stand exposed to you.*
> *Perhaps I am the found voice*
> *Of his eternal funk.*
> *Perhaps it's time to simply be,*
> *And put my plaint away.*
> *I guess he didn't love me.*
> *Maybe all the rest is bunk.*

She dropped her head to indicate she was finished, and
stood that way for a moment, before she raised her eyes and
began her second poem. The evening eventually ended.
I remembered a line from Swinburne: "even the weariest
river, winds somewhere safe to sea." I got up and bought a
copy of the poems, which appeared to have been run off on a
computer and bound in gray cardboard.

At home I had a large drink and sat at my kitchen counter and drank my drink and looked at her first poem.

Two painted ladies.

If I asked her about it, she'd give me a lot of grad-school razzmatazz about meaning and beauty. I wondered how she'd deal with a Middlesex County prosecutor.

57

We gathered in Kate Quaggliosi's office. Rosalind, me, Healy, and Belson as an interested observer. Rosalind immediately latched onto Kate, the other woman in a room with several men. My guess was that whatever her off-duty gender, in here she wasn't a woman, she was a prosecutor.

"My home was burglarized," she said.

"You report it to the Walford police?" Kate said.

"Yes."

"They take anything?"

"No, but I feel dreadfully invaded."

"Who would have done such a thing?" Healy said.

I looked at Healy. His face was expressionless.

"I've lost my husband," she said to Kate. "I am still very fragile."

Kate nodded and held up a copy of the painted-ladies poem.

"Walford cops are your best bet," she said. "Could you explain to me what this poem means, with particular attention to the two painted ladies?"

"I do not explain my poetry," Rosalind said. "A poem should not mean but simply be."

"I'm sure that's true," Kate said, "in English departments all across this great land. I'm sure it was true for Mr. McLeish, when he said it. Or something like it. But this is a homicide investigation, and in this arena it is not so."

Rosalind stared at her as if she'd uttered blasphemy.

"Something like it?" Rosalind said.

"If I remember my modern poetry seminar at BC," Kate said, "it was, 'A poem should not mean/But be.'"

"Oh, no," Rosalind said. "I'm sure Archie used the word 'simply.'"

"Sure," Kate said. "So what about these painted ladies?"

Rosalind looked as if she was disappointed in Kate. She glanced at me. I tried to look encouraging. She looked at Healy. He remained as expressionless as gray paint.

"I'm an artist," Rosalind said. "I do not cast my language before swine."

"And I'm an AD," Kate said. "And I might put your ass in jail."

"Jail?" Rosalind said.

"Jail," Kate said.

"For writing a poem?"

"For obstructing justice by refusing to divulge informa-tion needed in the investigation of your husband's death," Kate said.

Healy stood.

"You want me to arrest her?" he said to Kate.

Kate looked at Rosalind.

"Your choice," she said.

Had I been Rosalind, I'd have brought a lawyer with me. I suspected that Kate and Healy were on shaky legal ground, and a lawyer might have made that point. But Rosalind didn't have a lawyer, and that was all to the good. She got scared.

"I didn't . . ." she said. "I wasn't . . . I'll tell you anything you wish."

Healy sat back down and crossed his legs.

"Excellent," Kate said. "Did the reference to painted ladies have anything to do with the Hermenszoon painting that is missing?"

Two bright red smudges appeared on Rosalind's cheek-bones. She was taking in a lot of air. She seemed to be gather-ing herself. Kate waited. Healy and I watched.

"He cheated on me compulsively," Rosalind said. "He said he was addicted to sex."

"Lot of that going around," Kate said.

"I'm not sure he loved me at all," Rosalind said. "Though he said he did, and I stayed with him, because all my other choices were worse."

She breathed for a moment.

"But we used to talk, we'd known each other a long time, and it was, at worst, like a long habit, you know."

It was interesting how, as she got to talking about matters of personal substance, all the phony-accent artistic gobbledygook with which she'd plastered herself over went away. She seemed, for the moment, almost real.

"He always said he'd make it up to me," she said. "He always said he was going to make a lot of money, and we could live as we deserved to."

"How was he going to do that?" Kate said.

"He said he was going to swap the paintings."

"Which paintings."

"He had a good copy of *Lady with a Finch*," she said. "He was going to replace the real one with it. Then he'd have the original painting, and make some money, too."

"And he was the identifying expert," I said.

"So where is either of these paintings?" Kate said.

"The fraud," Rosalind said, "as in the poem, is on view in my home. As am I."

"You're a fraud, too?" Kate said.

"I was faithful to my husband," she said. "He was unfaithful to me. I was one half of a fraudulent relationship."

"I'd say that made him a fraud," Kate said.

Rosalind shrugged. She was slipping back into her poetic persona.

"It's a metaphor," she said.

"I have a question," I said.

She nodded at me without much warmth.

"How do you know the one in your house is a fake?"

"Well, it certainly isn't the original," she said.

"How do you know?"

"Why, we couldn't . . ." She paused. "Ashton told me it was."

"We could get somebody over there from the Hammond," Healy said.

"Their expert was Prince," I said.

"Someplace," Healy said.

"Guy in New York," I said.

"Gimme a name and address," Kate said. "We'll see if we can arrange it."

Rosalind stood.

"I wish to go now," she said.

"Sure," Kate said. "Just so long as I can find you when I want you."

"I'll be at home," she said.

"I can have someone drive you home," Kate said.

Rosalind shook her head.

"No," she said, and left.

"Show us," Kate said. "She don't need no stinking ride."

"I think there's more to get from her," Healy said.

"I do, too," Kate said. "But we pretty well used her up today. We'll have a few more rounds with her."

"Yeah," Healy said. "Telling the truth exhausted her."

"She's not used to it," I said. "She's been pretending all her life."

"You saw the painting," Healy said. "What do you think?"

"Looks good to me," I said. "But I don't count."

"How'd you get to see it?" Kate said.

"He B-and-E'd her house," Healy said.

"I never heard that," Kate said.

58

Susan took power yoga in a gym in Wellesley on Saturday mornings. I normally went with her and lifted some weights, and when she was though we'd go to breakfast. This morning I'd picked her up at nine-ten and we headed out the Mass Pike.

"People pick the damnedest ways to confess," I said.

"If they need to," Susan said.

"Rosalind confesses in her public poetry," I said. "Prince confesses in his doctoral dissertation."

"You should read mine," Susan said.

"Maybe I ought to."

"Be the first human to do so," Susan said. "Do you have any theory on how this swindle was supposed to work?"

"I've been dwelling on that," I said.

"Wow," Susan said. "Dwelling."

"For instance, I'm wondering how long this scheme has been incubating. He had to know for quite a while that *Lady with a Finch* was at the Hammond."

"And his father had, at one time, had possession of it," Susan said.

"And perhaps some claim on it," I said. "Or a claim that someone like Prince could persuade himself of. And he had a connection to the other claimants."

"The Herzberg family," Susan said.

"Which appears to consist primarily of Ariel Herzberg," I said. "And the family business seems to be finding art taken during the Holocaust and returning it to its rightful owner."

"So do you have a theory?" Susan said.

"Maybe Prince sought out the Herzbergs," I said, "citing the historical relationship, and suggested that they steal the painting. He'd authenticate it; they'd get the ransom and split it with him. Maybe he agreed to authenticate a phony, which he could get, being as how it was in his home, so they could get the ransom, keep the original, and probably keep it in the rightful possession of the Herzberg family."

"And they agreed?" Susan said.

"Say they did, and they stole it. And say that Prince wanted the ransom and the original painting. For whatever reason, including obsession. And he devised a way to swap them, he being the only one involved who could actually tell the real from the phony, and suppose they discovered his plan?" I said.

"How?"

"I don't know; maybe I'll never know. But Rosalind would not be my first choice of someone to share a mortal secret with."

"You think she might have blabbed?"

"Or written a poem, or told someone in confidence."

"So they went ahead with the ransom plan, and then blew him up," Susan said.

"And the painting, maybe," I said. "It at least casts doubt as to its whereabouts, and even its existence."

We were on Route 16 in Wellesley now. Susan was silent for a time as we drove in Saturday-morning traffic, past the handsome homes and the affluent shops.

Then she said, "You know there is a note of obsession running through this story."

"Yep."

"I mean, the Herzberg Foundation has a laudable mission," she said. "But two generations removed from the Holocaust, they end up killing people, and trying to kill you."

"They might argue that for a Jew, there is no removal from the Holocaust."

"They might," Susan said. "I would understand that."

"And how would you respond?" I said.

"No one may kill you," Susan said. "For whatever reason."

"That seems a good standard," I said.

"You will have trouble," Susan said, "proving all of this."

"Or any," I said. "Best bet is still to lure him into coming after me, and catching him in the act."

"Having first prevented him from killing you," Susan said.

"That first," I said. "But if we got him for attempted murder, we got something. Attempted murder carries pretty good time. Even if we never get him for Prince."

"Or the superintendent in your building."

"We'll get him for something," I said.

"Unless he gets you," Susan said.

"No one has," I said.

"I know," Susan said. "I know."

59

The next morning while I was in my office with the desk drawer open and one eye on my office door, the phone rang. It was Belson.

"Kate Quaggliosi called me, said there was a crime scene in Walford she thought I should see."

"Who?" I said.

"Rosalind," he said. "Want to ride along?"

"I do," I said.

"Ten minutes," Belson said. "Pick you up on Berkeley."

Which he did. We drove out Commonwealth Ave.

"Scenic route?" I said.

"No rush," he said. "Route Thirty all the way. Any traffic problems, I'll hit the siren."

"She dead?" I said.

"That's what they tell me," Belson said.

"Cause of death?" I said.

"Gunshot."

"They shut her up," I said.

"Imagine so," Belson said.

The traffic was backed up at North Harvard Street in Brighton with cars trying to turn. Belson sounded the siren. The waters parted, and we drove on through.

"Magic," I said.

"I always like that," Belson said.

When we got to Walford, there were half a dozen Walford and state police cruisers, a crime scene truck, a vehicle from the Middlesex coroner's office, and a couple of unmarked cars parked outside. There was also a considerable clump of civilians standing on the sidewalk, watching. A Walford cop stood at the front door, Belson showed him a badge, and the cop nodded and looked at my humble self.

"He's with me," Belson said.

"Go ahead," the cop said.

Inside, there were cops and photographers and Kate Quaggliosi. The Walford cops were trying to act as though a murder was nothing new to them. For the two state detectives, murder was nothing new. The ME squatted on the floor next to the body, and Kate Quaggliosi stood next to him, looking down.

"Mind if we take a look," Belson said to Kate.

He was always very punctilious about whose investigation it was.

"Be my guest," Kate said.

If the corpse bothered her, she didn't show it.

Belson and I sat on our haunches beside the ME.

"Took a pretty good beating before she died," Belson said.

The ME nodded.

"Two?" Belson said. "In the forehead?"

"Yep," the ME said. "One exit wound. The other one probably ricocheted around in the skull for a while."

"Close range?"

"Very," the ME said.

"When?" Belson said.

"Sometime last night," the ME said.

"Gee, thanks," Kate Quaggliosi said. "I saw her late yesterday afternoon. And her Pilates trainer found her at nine this morning. I could tell it was last night."

"He asked," the ME said. "We get her on the table, I'll be able to tell you a lot more."

"She's wearing the same clothes she had on at our meeting," Kate said.

"Probably makes it early evening," the ME said. "Before she put on her jammies."

"Anything you want to ask, Spenser?" Kate said.

"Her nose broken?" I said to the ME.

"Looks like it," he said. "Doesn't it."

"They musta wanted her to tell them something she didn't know," I said.

"Yes," Kate said. "She'd have given it up quick enough if she could."

Healy came in and walked over and looked at the body.

"Guess we didn't do her any favors having her in for a talk yesterday," he said.

"You think there's a connection?" Kate said.

"Yes," Healy said, looking down. "They really pounded on her. Anything missing?"

I looked at him. He looked at me. I stood.

"I'll check," I said, and walked into Prince's old office.

When I came out, I said, "Painting's gone."

"Real one?" Healy said.

"No way to know," I said.

"Why would they take a copy?" Kate said.

"Maybe they didn't," I said.

"You mean the genuine *Lady with a Finch*," Kate said, "might have been hanging in this guy's home office all this time?"

"Maybe," I said.

"Maybe Prince made the switch sooner than anyone thought," Healy said.

"Or maybe they weren't sure if he had or not," I said.

"And took this painting, to be sure," Kate said.

We were all silent for a while.

"We got more information in this case than we know what to do with," Belson said. "And we can't even make an arrest."

"Be nice if we could turn somebody," Kate said.

"Maybe we can," I said.

60

Molly Pitcher was wearing a little white blouse with a little Peter Pan collar and a little black string tie. Adorable.

"Morton Lloyd," I said.

"Do you have"—she looked up and her voice trailed off—"an appointment?"

"I do," I said, and walked past her into Lloyd's office carrying a manila envelope.

"What the hell are you doing," he said.

"I'm barging in," I said.

"Well, barge the hell right back out," Lloyd said.

"I'm hoping to save your life," I said.

"What?" Lloyd said.

I closed the door behind me.

"You know Rosalind Wellington?" I said.

"I don't really know her," he said. "I know she's Ashton Prince's wife. What's this about saving my life?"

"Would you recognize her if you saw her?" I said.

"I don't think I ever met her. Why are you asking?"

I took three of the goriest crime scene photos of the dead Rosalind out of the manila envelope and spread them faceup on his desk.

"What she looks like currently," I said.

He glanced down.

"Jesus Christ," he said. "What the hell are you doing?"

"That's Rosalind Wellington, the late wife of the late Ashton Prince," I said.

"She's dead."

"Yep. Somebody beat the hell out of her, then shot her twice in the forehead," I said.

"I don't want to look at this," he said.

"Shooting somebody in the forehead twice," I said, "is like wearing suspenders and a belt."

"Who did it?"

"We think it was the Herzberg Foundation," I said. "We think they killed her because she had information that might hurt them. And now we're worried about you."

"That Herzberg will kill me?"

"Yep."

He was silent, looking at me with an odd expression. It might have been fear. I walked to the window on the side wall of his office, the one that overlooked Batterymarch.

"Who's 'we'?" he said.

"Me and the cops," I said.

"Why aren't they here?"

"Figure if you're seen talking to the cops, you're a dead man," I said. "So they sent me."

I continued to look out the window.

"Who would see me?" he said.

I nodded out the window.

"Maybe them," I said.

He stood and came to the window. A silver BMW sedan with tinted windows was parked in a tow zone on Batterymarch.

"How do you know someone's in it," Lloyd said.

"Motor's running," I said. "See the vapor from the exhaust?"

"So probably some guy waiting for his wife or something," Lloyd said.

"They followed me here," I said.

Lloyd was silent. I glanced at him. His face seemed pale. He swallowed a couple of times.

"What are you gonna do?" Lloyd said.

He sounded as if his mouth was dry and talking was hard.

"I was thinking of asking you to tell me what you know about the Herzberg Foundation."

"And if I don't tell you?"

"I leave," I said. "What else can I do."

"They'll kill me," he said.

"If you talk?" I said.

"Yes."

"And if you don't," I said.

"Whaddya mean?" he said.

"There's a leak sprung somewhere in their enterprise," I said. "They're running around trying to button everything up. You know stuff. Button, button."

"Don't you even care?"

"Not especially," I said.

"You can't leave me alone," he said.

"Can, too," I said.

"I need protection," he said.

"Cops can give you that," I said. "If you got anything to give them."

He stared down at the BMW.

"Okay," he said. "Will you stay with me till the cops get here?"

"I will," I said. "And beyond."

"I don't want to go to jail," he said.

"Not my department," I said. "But the cops and the prosecutors generally don't like to put cooperative witnesses away. It discourages other cooperative witnesses."

"You got a gun?" he said.

"Yes."

He stared down at the BMW some more.

"And you'll stay with me until they get here," he said. "I can pay you."

"Coin of the realm here is information," I said. "I'll protect you."

"Okay," he said. "Call them."

About ten minutes after I called, Quirk and Belson walked into the office with a couple of uniformed cops. I could see a little color come back into Lloyd's face. The uniforms stayed in the outer office, to protect us. Belson followed Lloyd into the inner office.

"Who's in the Beamer," I said to Quirk.

"Lee Farrell," Quirk said. "It's his car."

"Tell him he does a good ominous," I said.

Quirk grinned, and we went into Lloyd's office, too.

61

I f you don't mind," Quirk said, "I'd like to tape this interview."

"I don't mind," Lloyd said.

Quirk took a tape recorder out of his briefcase and put it on the desk between him and Lloyd. He punched up record and put some identity on it, then nodded at Lloyd.

Lloyd looked at the recorder as if it made him uncomfortable.

"I'm not sure where to begin," Lloyd said.

Lloyd was changing shape before my very eyes. The presence of the cops probably helped him feel safer. And he was probably heartened by his own decision to tell what he knew. In any case, he no longer seemed frightened. He seemed, actually, sort of dignified.

"What's your relation to the Herzberg Foundation?" Quirk said.

"Legal counsel," Lloyd said.

"Why do they need a legal counsel?" Quirk said.

Lloyd smiled and clasped his hands behind his head and leaned back in his swivel chair.

"Everyone needs a legal counsel, Captain," he said.

Quirk nodded.

"Everybody I meet," Quirk said. "How did you get to be legal counsel to the Herzberg Foundation?"

"It's a tad circuitous," Lloyd said. "I am on the board at the Hammond Museum. Through that position, I came to know Ashton Prince. And it was through Ashton that I met Ariel Herzberg."

"What did you counsel him about," Quirk said.

"The mission of the Herzberg Foundation," Lloyd said, "is to locate objets d'art confiscated by the Nazis during the Holocaust, and to restore them to their rightful owners. As you might imagine, the question of rightful ownership, after all this time, is complex. I was asked to research the legality of possession and advise them of their rights in this matter."

"What if they can't find the rightful owner?" Quirk said.

"I believe in that case, once all possibilities are exhausted, they donate it to a museum or another appropriate entity."

"You on retainer?" Quirk said.

"No, this was pro bono," Lloyd said.

"Why?"

"Why pro bono?"

Quirk nodded.

"You're not known for it," he said.

"I'm Jewish," Lloyd said.

"I could tell by the name," Quirk said.

Lloyd smiled.

"My grandfather's name was Loydjeviche," Lloyd said. "When he got to Ellis Island, the immigration officers Americanized it."

"And you worked pro bono because you believed in the cause?" Quirk said.

"You're Irish," Lloyd said.

Quirk nodded.

"My grandfather's name was Quirk," he said.

"You cannot, probably, know what the Holocaust means to a person of Jewish heritage."

"I can learn," Quirk said.

It was always a pleasure to watch Quirk do an interview. He was pleasant, calm, implacable, and patient. One had the feeling he'd be perfectly happy to sit there and ask you questions until Flag Day. He showed emotion only when it served his interest to show it. And when he did, its contrast to the patience-of-Job posture was very effective. He was one of the two best I knew. If it weren't that I had the edge in charm and physical beauty, he'd have been as good as I was.

"My grandfather was lucky. He got out with his family,"

Lloyd said. "And I am here. And I am lucky. I feel that way quite keenly," he said. "Every day."

"You religious?" Quirk said.

"No," Lloyd said. "But I'm Jewish."

Quirk was silent for a moment.

Then he said, "Were you able to help them?"

"I amassed a considerable precedent file, and I was prepared to litigate for them if it came to that."

"How many art pieces have they rescued," Quirk said.

Lloyd sat still for a moment.

"I don't know," he said finally. "*Lady with a Finch* has pretty well preoccupied them since I've been aboard."

"Do you know where that is?" Quirk said.

"If it is not blown up, no," Lloyd said.

"Have they always been here?" Quirk said.

"No," Lloyd said. "When Ashton introduced me, he told me they'd just moved here from New Jersey and rented the place in Brighton."

"He say why they moved?"

"No, but I always assumed it was about *Lady with a Finch,*" Lloyd said.

Quirk leaned over and checked the tape recorder, listened to a moment of playback, nodded to himself, set it back down, and pushed record again.

"Tell me about Ariel Herzberg," Quirk said.

"His grandfather was not lucky," Lloyd said. "I believe he died in Auschwitz, where Ariel's father spent several years of his childhood."

"Nine to fourteen," I said.

Everybody looked at me as if I had barged onto the stage during a performance.

"When he was liberated," Lloyd went on, "his only possession was *Lady with a Finch*. Which he sold to a dealer in Rotterdam right after the war. The question Ariel wanted answered, with which I was trying to help, was: Did the sale constitute a legal agreement among adults? I thought we could certainly argue that it did not. The boy was fourteen and destitute, recently free after five years in Auschwitz, with no legal guardian. It was our position that the dealer exploited the boy, and that all else in terms of legal possession is tainted by that initial illegality."

"Who's financing all this?" Quirk said.

"I don't know," Lloyd said. "The foundation seems to have enough money."

"Didn't you have to lend them a car?" Quirk said, as if he was puzzled.

Lloyd smiled.

"That, I think, had more to do with low profile," he said, "than money."

I glanced at Belson. He seemed to be sitting blankly, looking at Lloyd. But I knew he heard every word.

"They do any fund-raising?" Quirk said.

"No, I don't think so," Lloyd said. "I offered to introduce them to philanthropic members of the Jewish community, but they said they didn't want to be beholden."

Quirk nodded.

"But they had money," Quirk said.

"Apparently," Lloyd said.

"Do you know where they got it?"

"No," Lloyd said.

Quirk nodded again.

"Tell me more about Ariel," he said. "Did you think his dedication was real?"

"To the point of obsession," Lloyd said.

"Would he kill someone?"

"Kill someone?" Lloyd said. "He's trying to do good."

"So he wouldn't kill anybody?" Quirk said.

"No," Lloyd said. "Good God, of course not."

"So what are you scared of?" Quirk said.

I smiled to myself.

Gotcha.

Lloyd was silent. It wasn't a silence of pondering the question. It was a silence of *I don't know what to say.* He had relaxed as he talked, feeling more and more lawyerly, confident that he could play these cops. Quirk was patient. He waited, letting the pressure of the silence work on Lloyd.

"This seemed personal to him," Lloyd said finally.

"Enough to kill people?"

Lloyd contemplated his answer for a bit.

Then he said, "If you knew too much."

"You know too much?" Quirk said.

"I know what I've told you."

"You think he killed others?"

"Prince, and Prince's wife, maybe," Lloyd said. "A building supervisor in a building on Marlborough Street."

"Because they knew too much?"

"Maybe," Lloyd said.

"What did they know too much about?" Quirk said.

"This damn painting," Lloyd said.

"*Lady with a Finch?*" Quirk said.

"Yes."

"And you?" Quirk said.

"I guess I might know too much about the organization."

"What?" Quirk said.

"Several former Israeli commandos work for the foundation."

"How many?"

"Don't know," Lloyd said. "I just know that a couple of them often accompany Ariel. I think they are armed."

"See any tattoos?" Quirk said.

"Yes, some of them, those where I could see it, have a number tattooed on their forearm. Ariel has it, too."

"Know any names?" Quirk said.

"No," Lloyd said. "I don't think so."

"Joost?" Quirk said. "Or Van Meer?"

"No, I . . . Joost," he said. "There was a baseball player. . . ."

"Eddie Joost," I said.

"Yes. I don't remember him, but my father was a big fan of his," Lloyd said. "I think he liked the name, mostly."

"And this other guy Joost worked for the Herzberg Foundation?"

"Yes," Lloyd said. "Is it important?"

"I think it might be," Quirk said.

He looked at Belson.

"Frank," he said, "I'll look after Mr. Lloyd. Why don't you take some people and go get Mr. Herzberg."

Belson nodded. He stood and glanced at me.

"Want to ride along?" he said.

"I'd be a fool not to," I said.

62

An apprehension team, wearing vests and helmets with face masks and sitting in an unmarked van, met us in the parking lot at District 14 Station on Washington Street. They were under the command of a sergeant who looked as though he might floss with a crowbar.

The sergeant looked at me and said, "Who's this?"

"My bodyguard," Belson said. "You've looked at the site?"

"Yeah."

"I want the building covered on all four," Belson said. "I want the guys at each corner of the property in visual contact with the guy at the corners on each side of him. You've done this before."

"Sure," the sergeant said. "One question. Your buddy here a cop, or we gotta take care of him?"

"He'll take care of himself," Belson said. "Let's get to it."

The apprehension team went first, and we followed. They pulled up in front of the Herzberg Foundation and poured out of the car. In thirty seconds they had the place surrounded. Two guys with a short ram stood by the front door. The sergeant looked at Belson and nodded.

Frank and I went up the stairs and tried the door. It was open. Frank and I both took out our guns and went in. Nothing. The place throbbed with emptiness. No people. No papers. No coffeepots. No water bottles. Neat, clean, and deserted.

"Balls," Belson said.

"Exactly," I said.

Belson looked at the command sergeant.

"Make sure," Belson said.

The sergeant nodded, and the team searched the house. It was as empty as it felt.

"They been a step ahead of us pretty much all along," Belson said. "How'd they know."

"Might be my fault," I said.

"They decided to bail after you told them how much you knew?" Belson said.

"I was trying to bait him, get him to do something hasty," I said.

Belson nodded.

"Case like this," Belson said, "there's not that much choice. You poke and push and see what happens. Better than doing nothing."

"This time what happened is that they took off," I said.

"Maybe," Belson said. "Maybe something else."

The sergeant came back and reported that the building was empty.

"Okay," Belson said. "Canvass the neighborhood, see if you can learn anything."

The sergeant nodded.

"When they left, how they left, where they went, whatever," Belson said.

"We're on it," the sergeant said.

"And take off the armor so your people don't scare the neighbors to death."

The sergeant grinned.

"Some of my people look better with the armor on," he said.

While the neighborhood was being canvassed, Belson and I walked through the building, opening drawers, looking in wastebaskets. We didn't find anything.

"Could get the scientists in here," Belson said.

"Prints?" I said.

"Whatever," Belson said.

"It appears to me that this place was rented furnished," I said.

"So there might be quite a few prints?" Belson said.

"An embarrassment of riches," I said.

"You're probably right," Belson said. "But I'll have them take a look, anyway. Makes them feel important."

The sergeant came back into the building.

"Left a couple days ago," he said. "Took a few boxes. In

some kind of rental van. One guy thinks it might have been a Ryder. Nobody got an idea where they went."

"I'll check the rental van," Belson said. "We'll see who owns this building and who they rented it to. Something might turn up."

"So you don't need us no more, we'll pack up and go home," the sergeant said.

"Thanks for stopping by," Belson said.

The sergeant looked at me.

"You carry a gun," he said. "I seen you take it out when you went in the house."

"Seemed like a good idea at the time," I said.

"You ain't a cop," he said.

"Not anymore," I said.

"He's a private license," Belson said. "He's been working on this case longer than I have."

The sergeant nodded.

"Just asking," he said.

When he was gone, I said, "Alert to any transgression."

Belson nodded.

"Probably make lieutenant before I do," Belson said.

"Might help," I said, "if you take the lieutenant's exam."

"Fuck the lieutenant's exam," Belson said.

"Your position remains consistent," I said.

"Ain't gonna change," Belson said. "I've been a cop a long time. I don't need to prove myself in some fucking exam."

"You do if you want to make lieutenant," I said.

"Fuck lieutenant, too," Belson said.

I grinned.

"No wonder we get along," I said.

Belson looked at me without expression.

"Who says we get along?" Belson said.

63

If you didn't know you were Jewish," I said, "would you know you were Jewish?"

Susan looked at me carefully.

"Is this a trick question?" she said.

We were in bed. Having completed the more rambunctious part of our evening together, we had invited Pearl into the bedroom. She had tried to settle in between Susan and me, but I outmuscled her, and she settled for the foot of the bed. Dogs are adaptive.

"No," I said. "I know you're not religious. And your ancestors came from Germany. But . . ."

"But I'm Jewish," Susan said. "I'm a Jew in the same way I'm a woman. It is who and what I am."

"And if you didn't know?" I said.

"I don't believe in magic," Susan said. "Although there are moments in a therapy session . . . No. No more so than I can speak Hebrew. The irony about Jewishness, I've always thought, is that it has been intensified by repression."

"Containment enhances the power of explosion," I said.

"Something like that," Susan said.

Our earlier rambunctiousness had pretty well done away with the bedcovers. Susan made a weak effort at modesty by pulling one edge of the comforter over her thighs. She had been doing power yoga for some time now, and was pleased with her strength and flexibility. As she talked, she raised one naked leg and pointed it toward the ceiling, which pretty well took care of the modesty issue.

"Flexible," I said.

"And strong," she said.

"Good traits in a woman," I said.

She smiled and raised the other leg. Pearl eyed the space that had been created but stayed put. I eyed her both legs pointing at the ceiling.

"Also comely," I said.

"Jewesses are frequently comely," Susan said.

"None as comely as you," I said.

Susan flexed her elevated ankles.

"Doubtless," she said.

"This thing with the paintings has been the most Jewish thing I've ever dealt with."

"Except me," Susan said.

"As always," I said. "There's you, and there's everybody else."

"All the bad guys appear to be Jewish," Susan said.

"I'm beginning to feel like an anti-Semite," I said.

Susan, with both legs still sticking up in the air, turned from admiring them to look at me.

"You're not," she said.

"I know," I said. "Now, if I could just find Ariel Herzberg."

Susan put her legs down, which was good news and bad news. The good news was I could think of something else. It was also the bad news.

"What is he like?" Susan said.

"I don't know. I have no handle on him. I thought I could lure him into trying to kill me, and instead I lured him into disappearing."

"Disappearing may be a bit solipsistic," Susan said. "He's not disappeared. He's someplace. You just don't know where."

"My God," I said. "I'm in bed with Noah Webster."

"Think about it," Susan said. "Worst case. He's on the run. He's alone. He has to go somewhere. If you were at the end of your rope and in his situation, where would you go?"

"To you," I said.

Susan nodded.

"Does he have a me?"

"No one does," I said.

"You know what I mean," she said. "There's an ex-wife. There's a daughter."

"Ex-wife doesn't hold him in high esteem," I said.

"'Home is where, when you have to go there, they have to take you in,'" Susan said.

"It's not Noah Webster," I said. "It's Robert Frost."

"When people run," Susan said, "they run home."

"And the daughter thinks he's heroic," I said.

"It'll be the wife," Susan said.

"How do you know?"

"Shrink, woman, and comely Jewess," Susan said.

"Oh," I said. "That's how."

64

Bright and early, while the coffee was brewing in my office pot, I called Crosby at Walford.

"Can you see if you can locate Missy Minor?" I said.

"You want me to hold her?"

"I don't even want her to know you located her. Just let me know."

"I'll be surreptitious," he said.

"You don't sound like a cop," I said. "You got to stop hanging around the faculty lounge."

"Oh, okay," Crosby said. "I'll be fucking surreptitious."

"Better," I said.

I hung up and dialed Shawmut Insurance and asked for Winifred Minor. *She was not in today.* I asked if she was ill. *That information was not available.* Of course it wasn't. I hung up and checked the coffee. It was ready, so I poured some and added milk and sugar and sat down with it. I was on my second cup when Crosby called back.

"She don't answer the bell at her dorm," he said when I picked up the phone. "And she isn't at the gym or anywhere like that."

"And what were you going to say if she did answer the door?" I said.

"I told my guy to say, 'There's been a burglary in one of the dorms and we're just warning all the members of the Walford community.'"

"Slick," I said. "Might she be in class?"

"Only class today is twelve to three," he said. "We'll check when the time comes, let you know."

"You know any of her friends?" I said.

"Don't know any," Crosby said. "Can find out. But I'd have to start asking around, and that's not surreptitious."

"True," I said.

"Something cooking?" he said.

"If only I knew," I said.

"Happy to help," he said. "If I can. It's almost like police work."

"Thanks, Crosby," I said.

"No problem, pal."

"Anyone ever call you Bing?"

"No," he said.

After we hung up, I sat and drank coffee and thought. Several doughnuts would have helped that process, but Susan had convinced me they were not nourishing, and I was trying to be loyal to her. Love is not always a simple thing.

He was there. I was convinced of that. What I was thinking about was what to do about it. I didn't know if he was there holding them hostage, or if he was there being clasped to the bosom of his family. I didn't want the cops, at least until I knew what the arrangement was. Once the cops are in, you no longer control anything. I wanted to keep Winifred and Missy out of it, if I could.

I finished my coffee and stood up.

Time to reconnoiter.

65

Winifred Minor's address was one of the palisade of condos that had gone up in the old navy yard after the navy moved mostly out. There was still a small presence fenced off at the city square end of the yard, but the rest was residential. There were some small shops to service the residents, but most of the effort and money had been expended on the waterfront, where you could look out your window at harbor traffic, and across the harbor at Boston.

Winifred lived in a gray clapboard town house at the end of a long corridor of gray clapboard town houses, all of which were elevated a level to permit parking underneath. This meant climbing a significant stairway and walking along a deck in front of the town houses until you found the number you wanted.

On the way over from my office I had carefully thought out the options for gaining entry, once I had scoped the place out a little. I reviewed my options as I climbed the stairs and moved down the deck. Winifred was located three from the water end of the row. The option I chose was breathtaking in its simplicity.

I rang the bell.

In an appropriate amount of time, Winifred opened the door. She opened it only a little, enough to see out. And when she saw me she stood and stared, with one hand on the open edge of the door.

"May I come in?" I said.

She blinked a couple of times, as if the question was too hard for her.

Then she said, "No, no, I don't think so. We're busy now."

"How about I wait?" I said.

She shook her head.

"No," she said. "We'll be busy all day."

I nodded. Her face was stiff. But as I looked at her, she glanced down at the door lock where her hand rested, and as I looked down with her, she pushed in the little button that kept the door from locking automatically when it was closed.

"Perhaps I could come back tomorrow," I said.

"Suit yourself," Winifred said, and closed the door.

I pressed my ear against it and heard her steps receding up the stairs. I stayed where I was for a moment and then gently tried the thumb latch on the door. It was open. I went in very quietly and eased the door shut behind me. I was in a small hallway that led to a sitting room with a big window that looked out on the harbor. The room was furnished as an office. To the left, a stairway led up to what I assumed were the living quarters.

Vertical architecture.

I had a Smith & Wesson .40-caliber on my hip, and a short-barreled .38 in an ankle holster. But if there was shooting in the kind of space I seemed to be in, then Winifred and Missy were at risk. Me, too, but I had signed on for it. I was wearing jeans and sneakers, a black T-shirt, and a leather jacket. The T-shirt had a little pocket on the chest. I took off the leather jacket and put it on the floor. I took the S&W off my hip and cocked it, and held it a little behind my right thigh and started quietly up the steps.

And there he was. Sitting in an armchair, drinking a glass of orange juice. His daughter sat in a straight chair near him. And his ex-wife sat on the couch with her hands clasped tightly and resting on her knees.

"Ariel Herzberg," I said. "As I live and breathe."

His reaction time was excellent. He dropped the orange juice, came to his feet in one graceful movement, stepped behind Missy's chair, and produced a semiautomatic pistol.

Missy said, "Daddy?"

He made a push-away gesture at her.

I said, "Why don't you go over beside your mother, Missy."

"No," Ariel said. "Stay put."

Missy looked at her mother. Her mother put her hand up, palm out, in a stay-put gesture.

"You know why he wants you to stay?" I said.

"So I won't be caught in a crossfire," she said.

She was trying for defiance, but her voice was a little shaky.

"Pretty to think so," I said. "But he knows I will hesitate to shoot if you are there."

She looked at Ariel.

"Stay where you are," he said, without looking at her.

"For God's sake, Ariel," Winifred said. "She's your daughter. You can't use her as a shield. Even you."

"I do what needs to be done," he said. "I have always done what needed to be done."

Winifred stood.

"Where are you going?" Ariel said.

"If I can't protect my daughter, at least I can protect myself," she said, and walked across the living room and up the stairs.

"Remember," Ariel said, "I have the girl."

Winifred made no answer as she disappeared up the stairs.

"You have the girl?" Missy said.

"Shut up," Ariel said to her.

He was looking a little beleaguered, and as best I could see, he hadn't cocked the pistol.

"I've tried to kill you at least twice," he said. "You are

both skillful and lucky, and you have by and large destroyed my operation here."

"No need to thank me," I said.

Ariel shook his head slightly, as if there was something in his ear.

"But now I have you," he said.

"Somebody has somebody," I said. "And you haven't cocked your weapon."

Ariel smiled and thumbed back the hammer.

"You won't shoot," he said. "You won't risk hurting the girl."

He was right, and I knew it, and he knew that I knew it. I focused on his gun hand. As soon as it tightened I would dive, and maybe the girl could get out of the way before he killed me.

"Daddy," Missy said.

Her voice scraped out as if her throat was nearly shut.

"Be still," he said.

"You are hiding behind me," she rasped.

"I'll kill him," he said. "Then you and I will leave."

"You are going to hide behind me and shoot a man."

"I am," Ariel said, and raised the pistol.

I watched his hand. Missy stood up quite suddenly and lunged in front of me. I grabbed her and pushed her sprawling down behind the couch, and joined her. When we hit the floor, I shoved her away and rolled onto my stomach with my gun out ahead of me. The sound of a big flat shot filled the room, and Ariel stepped backward calmly and fell over on his back. I came to my feet and stepped around the couch to where Ariel lay on his back, his eyes open, seeing nothing. I crouched down and felt for his pulse, but I knew that there'd be no pulse. And there wasn't. I stood and looked up. Winifred was at the top of the stairs, holding a long-barreled rifle. She was crying. Behind the couch, Missy was crying and yelling, "Momma." She was struggling with her crying. "Momma." Still carrying the rifle, Winifred half ran, half fell down the stairs and dropped to her knees beside her daughter. She put the rifle down on the rug beside her and put her arms around Missy, and they rocked back and forth together on the floor behind the couch. I took my gun off cock and put it back on my hip. I went to the kitchen and found a bottle of scotch and a water glass. I got ice from the refrigerator, put the ice in the glass, and poured some scotch over it. Then I walked back into the living room. A big container ship went dreamily past the picture window, heading for the Mystic River. The women cried and rocked.

I found a big hassock and sat on it and sipped my scotch and was quiet.

66

They stopped crying and sat together on the floor behind the couch.

"We need to talk a little before the cops come," I said.

"Do they have to come?" Winifred said.

"Yes."

"I know," she said.

Winifred stood and put the rifle carefully on the long coffee table. Then she turned and put her hand out to Missy, and pulled her to her feet. Neither one looked at the dead man lying on the floor.

"Where did I hit him?" Winifred said.

"Middle of the mass," I said.

"I was the best shot in the Chicago office," she said. "He was going to take her."

"You shot him," Missy said.

Winifred nodded slowly.

"Yes," she said.

"Is he dead?" Missy said.

"Yes."

"Will they arrest you?" Missy said.

"I don't think so," Winifred said.

"No," I said. "They won't."

"I don't want to talk in here," Winifred said.

"Kitchen?" I said.

"Yes."

We sat at the kitchen table with the scotch bottle in front of us. Winifred got glasses and ice, and poured a drink for Missy and a drink for herself.

"Okay," I said. "The rifle legal?"

"Yes," Winifred said.

Missy sipped some scotch.

"He didn't love me," she said.

"He didn't have much in the way of feelings," Winifred said. "He might have cared more about you than anyone else."

"I thought he was a hero," Missy said. "Restoring not only things but honor to his people, helping to erase some of the stain of the Holocaust, all this time later."

"You're quoting him," Winifred said. "He used to say the same thing to me."

"What was he really doing?" I said.

"Stealing paintings and selling them."

"Tell me what you know," I said.

"Hell," Winifred said. "I know everything."

"He was stealing paintings?" Missy said.

"His father had been in the death camp. The offspring of Holocaust survivors often feel a need to atone for not having been part of it."

"Not being in the Holocaust?" Missy said.

"I've done a lot of reading on the subject," Winifred said. "And I think, in the beginning, the Herzberg Foundation was authentic. He was really trying to even up for the Holocaust. Take some risk to liberate objets d'art and restore them to their rightful owners."

"So if someone wouldn't sell him the work of art, he'd steal it," I said.

"Yes."

"And money became an issue, given the cost of buying such pictures."

"And he felt it was wrong that he should have to pay," Winifred said.

She poured a little more scotch into her glass.

"So he began to steal all of them," she said. "It was his right. And he began to sell a few of them to finance the foundation, which needed it."

"And it was working good," I said. "And after a while the foundation became an end, not a means."

"The foundation," Winifred said, "c'est moi."

"And the Auschwitz tattoos?" I said. "And the Israeli commandos? And the rest?"

"Whatever it started out as," Winifred said, "it became . . . It was set decoration."

I nodded.

"How do you know all this?" Missy said.

"Honey, I was a first-rate investigator," Winifred said. "I knew most of it in Chicago."

"And you let him . . ."

Winifred took her daughter's hand.

"Conceive you?" Winifred said. "Eagerly. You are not the only one who loved him foolishly."

"How about Ashton Prince?" I said.

"They were partners," Winifred said. "There was a family connection back to Auschwitz, I think. I'm not clear on the details. But Ashton would locate a painting, authenticate it, appraise it, and when they stole it and sold it, he would get a cut."

"Why did they kill him?" I said.

"Ariel said that Ashton was trying to cheat them."

"And he was afraid they'd catch him at it," I said, "which is why he brought me along to protect him. Do you know how he was planning to cheat them?"

"No."

I nodded.

"I think he was planning to switch paintings on them," I said. "You have any idea where *Lady with a Finch* might be?"

Winifred, still holding Missy's hand, tapped it gently against her own thigh. Her expression changed. If she had not been so recently traumatized, she might have smiled.

"In my bedroom closet," she said. "There's two of them."

67

We were standing near the George Washington statue that faced Arlington Street. It was March. There was still snow in the Public Garden, but it was diminishing. Of course, in Boston March is not necessarily blizzard-free, but the odds are better, and so far the odds were holding. We were waiting for Otto.

"His mom e-mailed me last night," Susan said. "They'll be in town, and she feels Otto is desperate to see Pearl."

"Why would he not be?" I said.

"I think it may be why they came up," Susan said.

Pearl was engaged stalking some pigeons about ten yards from us. The pigeons allowed her to get quite close before they scornfully took wing. She watched them fly and saw them land maybe thirty yards away, and started over to stalk them some more.

"She doesn't discourage easily," Susan said.

"Hell," I said. "The hunt is most of the fun."

"You should know," Susan said.

I nodded.

"Lotta trouble, though," I said. "Sometimes."

"Are the police going to charge either Winifred or Missy with anything?" Susan said.

"No, an armed man with a history of murder, holding her daughter as a shield? There's no case there. And no one wants to make one. It's self-defense."

Pearl got really low as she closed in on the pigeons, and almost got there before they flew up. She watched them carefully as they flew entirely out of the Public Garden and across Beacon Street, toward the esplanade.

"And the paintings?" Susan said.

"Both there. The cops are having them examined to see which is which."

Susan looked at her watch and looked toward Boylston Street, where she expected Otto to appear.

"Cops suspect that the copy might have been in the Hammond Museum, and that Prince had the real one on his wall."

"Do you think that's true?" Susan said.

"Might be," I said. "I'm not sure there's any way to know for sure."

"What got him killed?"

"Ariel said that Prince was going to cheat them. My guess is he'd authenticate the fake, collect the ransom, take his share, and put the real one back in his office."

"Could you prove that?"

"Maybe," I said. "If I had to. But I don't have to."

Susan glanced toward Boylston Street.

"What was Ariel's plan, do you suppose?" Susan said.

"Best we can figure, he was going to hole up there. He had the daughter convinced that he cared for her and was going to take her with him and the pictures when the heat had turned down."

"You don't think he would have?"

"The daughter was a way to make sure that Winifred behaved. If he didn't need her for that anymore, no. I don't think he'd have taken her. She would have been a bother."

"A father that would use his daughter as a shield . . ."

"Exactly," I said.

Pearl gave up on pigeons and came over and sat on my foot. She sat on my foot a lot, but always for reasons known only to her.

"It's hard to imagine," Susan said, "what he was about."

"Ariel?" I said.

"Yes. How much was sincere, at least at first, how much was traceable to being the child of a survivor."

"How much is traceable to his being emotionally barren," I said.

"That's almost your standard of good and bad," Susan said. "The ability to love."

"Probably," I said.

"The inability may be traceable to his history," she said.

"Probably is," I said. "But it did a lot of damage."

Susan nodded. Pearl stood up suddenly, her tail wagging very fast. She made little cooing noises.

"Speaking of the ability to love," I said.

Susan looked toward Boylston Street. And there he was, barreling across the Public Garden like a Cape buffalo.

Otto!